ALADDIN

ALADDIN

A New Translation

TRANSLATED BY YASMINE SEALE

EDITED BY PAULO LEMOS HORTA

LIVERIGHT PUBLISHING CORPORATION

A Division of W. W. Norton & Company

Independent Publishers Since 1923

New York • London

CONTENTS

INTRODUCTION

One of the world's most famous and beloved fairy tales, "Aladdin, or the Wonderful Lamp," has been retold and adapted time and time again since it first appeared in French in the early eighteenth century. It may seem surprising that a story so powerfully associated with the collection of Arabic tales known as the *Thousand and One Nights* should have come down to us through French—but it is also apt. The tale has never stopped traveling. Authors from Charles Dickens and Dante Gabriel Rossetti to Clarice Lispector and Salman Rushdie have written about their experiences of encountering the story as children. My own mother often regaled me with the story of her first encounter with the tale, as a six-year-old orphan receiving her first gift of the *Arabian Nights* from her adoptive father in the north of Brazil. Through the centuries, the tale's broad and lasting appeal rests on its ability to encompass both our wildest longings and our deepest uncertainties—both the childhood dream of wish fulfillment and the terrors of coming of age.

At the heart of the story is the mystery surrounding Aladdin himself. Why should he, a boy of little talent or ambition, have been chosen for the extraordinary adventures that await him? Why should he, rather than another, have the lamp?

In an attempt to answer this riddle, scholars and screenwriters alike have invented variations on the tale that have the boy perform some meritorious act to demonstrate that he deserves the lamp. Folklorists have identified precedents in Buddhist tales where characters save animals from danger and are rewarded with a wishing stone. The Disney film portrays Aladdin as a "diamond in the rough," forced by poverty to steal but generously giving to those who are less fortunate than himself. Others have argued that it is in fact the lamp that makes the man. Richard Francis Burton, the infamous adventurer and translator of the *Arabian Nights*, suggested that the lamp had the power to alter "the physique and morale of the owner" and therefore to transform the "raw" youth into "a finished courtier, warrior, statesman." The scholar Tzvetan Todorov sees Aladdin as part of a line of what he calls "narrative men," devoid of character other than the marvels and machinations of fate that work through them.

Like many a comic book hero—think of Peter Parker receiving a bite from a radioactive spider—Aladdin is transformed into the tale's hero by coming into possession of the lamp. Once in command of it, and its slave the jinni, Aladdin is no longer a passive recipient of magical good fortune but an agent of his own fate. The heroine of the story, the princess Badr al-Budur, is equally active in shaping its outcome, saving Aladdin's life by outwitting the magician in the tale's climax.

"Aladdin" has a peculiar relationship to the *Thousand and One Nights*. First added to the collection in the French translation produced by Antoine Galland in early eighteenth century Paris, the tale of "Aladdin" has not been found in any authentic Arabic manuscript predating this telling. Galland added the story, along with other tales such as "Ali Baba and the Forty Thieves," to his French collection, after running out of stories to translate from his Arabic manuscript of the *Thousand and One Nights*. In his diary, Galland claimed that a Maronite Christian traveler from Aleppo named Hanna Diyab told him these stories during a visit to Paris in 1709, and, in the case of "Aladdin," gave him a manuscript of the tale. While some scholars have doubted the existence of this mysterious Syrian storyteller, the recent discovery of Diyab's memoir chronicling his travels to Paris confirms that he both met the French translator and provided him with stories with which to complete his translation of the *Thousand and One Nights*.

Despite this revelation, fundamental questions regarding the origins of "Aladdin" remain unanswered. Whose story is Aladdin really? There is broad agreement that, compared to the original Arabic tales of the *Thousand and One Nights*, "Aladdin" and the other tales told to Galland by Diyab draw more heavily on the marvelous, in the sense of both material treasures and supernatural creatures and events. Some have attributed these differences to the imagination of the French Orientalist Galland, who used the raw material of a text of unknown provenance to channel his own conception of an exotic East. The novelist Marina Warner has pointed to the presence of popular eighteenth century storytelling elements—talismans, spoken charms, and the inversion of social order—as evidence of a French hand in Aladdin's composition. The discovery of Diyab's memoir, however, suggests that the gift of the tale to Galland was the product of the fertile imagination of a young Syrian Maronite raised within the storytelling culture of a caravan city. The novelist and Arabist Robert Irwin has argued that many of the elements identified as peculiar to a European narrative tradition in "Aladdin" have clear precedents in popular Arabic literature. The *Thousand and One Nights* contains other stories of lazy youths undeserving of their good fortune, and other characters who conjure jinn from rings and build palaces to woo the objects of their desire.

I find it intriguing to read the tale of Aladdin alongside

Diyab's record of his own youthful adventures as he jour-
neyed from Aleppo to Paris and the royal court at Versailles
in defiance of his family's wishes. The similarities between
the two narratives might help explain his attraction to the
tale that he provided to Galland, even if he did not have a
hand in its composition. The youngest of several brothers
who apprenticed with a French merchant in Aleppo, Hanna
Diyab understood the appeal of the magician's empty
promise to help Aladdin establish himself as a cloth merchant in the market. This magician, who lures Aladdin into
his service by pretending to be his uncle, carries echoes
of the French adventurer Paul Lucas, who enticed Diyab
to accompany him on a treasure-hunting journey through
the Mediterranean with the promise of a position at the
French court. Lucas's reputation rested on the various false
identities he assumed and on his purported skill in the use
of amulets and charms to heal ailments. In his memoir,
Diyab relates the Frenchman's claim that he could harness
the power of the philosopher's stone against the ravages of
age. Strangely enough, the first tomb-raiding expedition
that Diyab describes in his account of his time with Lucas
yielded both a ring and a lamp.

Diyab's description of his travels with Lucas bears the
mark of a confident storyteller, not averse to heightening
suspense by embedding a tale within another in the manner of Shahrazad. His account of the wonders of Versailles,
where he was presented to Louis XIV, contains phrases
that mirror the descriptions of palaces and princesses in

the stories of "Aladdin" and "Prince Ahmad," another tale added to the *Arabian Nights* thanks to Diyab. Not much older than the adolescent Aladdin when he visited Paris, Diyab reveals a sympathy for the impoverished and the persecuted during the harsh winter of 1708–9 and the famine that ensued in the following months. No surprise, then, that the tales he recounted to Galland in the spring of 1709 often revolve around the young and the socially marginal, not least the story of a poor boy whose life is transformed by the possession of a magical lamp.

Whether one attributes the story's appeal to the perspective of the young Syrian traveler or the learned French translator, "Aladdin" proved a timely response to the emerging thirst among the French reading public for fairy tales. Galland's *Les Mille et Une Nuits* was the publishing phenomenon of its day, arriving at the height of the Parisian craze for the *conte de fées*, and shaping all aspects of French taste in its wake, from stage sets to street fashion and interior design. Legend has it that impatient readers waiting for the next installment of the twelve-volume collection would pelt the windows of Galland's apartment with stones until he came out to relate a new tale. Galland himself protested in a letter that he was not overly fond of the genre, and he resented that his treatises on coins and coffee were not as popular. But the stories Diyab gave to Galland were remarkably well suited to the demands of the French publishing market at that moment. "Aladdin," alongside "Ali Baba" and "Prince Ahmad," would prove to be among the most enduringly popular stories from the *Arabian Nights*, circulating around the globe, from page to stage to screen. These added stories have become the lens through which European readers viewed the *Thousand and One Nights* as a whole. By adding Diyab's tales to the collection, Galland taught Europe to read the entire story collection as a repository of marvels.

English translations of "Aladdin" allowed it to circulate in a variety of new contexts. Even before Galland had finished his multi-volume translation in 1717, an anonymous "Grub Street" version of his *Arabian Nights* was being published in London, and "Aladdin" would take its place as part of this new world of popular publishing. By the early nineteenth century, English versions of the story were circulating in stand-alone chapbooks, in collections of *Arabian Nights* tales adapted for children, and in general anthologies of fairy tales, where the story might be bound together with an English fairy tale like "Jack and the Beanstalk." The abridged version of "Aladdin" for children published by Elizabeth Newbery in 1790 as part of *The Oriental Moralist* was carefully stripped of any element that "might give the least offence to the most delicate reader," and so this Aladdin has the vizier's son spend his lonely wedding night in a stable with clean straw rather than locked in a lavatory. In these popular children's editions, Aladdin had to offer an appropriate example of virtue for young minds.

Originally set in a nameless kingdom in China, the story of Aladdin was transposed to other settings in a never-ending cycle of adaptation. While illustrated editions of the story often gave flight to exotic fantasies of the Orient, Aladdin's adventures could also unfold in the streets of Paris or London. The uncertainties of the story's original sources were forgotten in popular pastiches where French palaces and scenes were used to illustrate vaguely Chinese landscapes. In nineteenth century England, to come across "Aladdin" as part of the *Thousand and One Nights* was the exception rather than the rule. The overwhelming majority of Victorian readers, like the majority of readers in English ever since, encountered "Aladdin" in adaptations for children.

As the popularity of "Aladdin" grew, in the late eighteenth century it made the leap onto the British stage, where it became one of the most frequently performed pantomimes of the Christmas season. As a pantomime, a theatrical entertainment for children involving music and comedy, "Aladdin" was transformed into a crowd-pleasing spectacle that exploited the exotic settings and the rapid shifts of fortune in the story: the version staged at Drury Lane in 1885 included a remarkable eleven scene changes. These productions, as well as other theatrical adaptations, brought the attention of early filmmakers to the story. The first films based on *Arabian Nights* stories were often simply filmed versions of the stage productions and extravaganzas that were already popular with the general public, often featuring the plots and characters added by Galland and Diyab to the *Nights*.

Long before Disney chose "Aladdin" as the basis for its

animated film of 1992, the tale was already an established global franchise. Connoisseurs of silent film will remember *The Thief of Bagdad*, the Douglas Fairbanks hit from 1924, which borrowed from "Aladdin," "Ali Baba," and "Prince Ahmad," but even before this Hollywood hit German studios were already exploring Oriental fantasies on film—in Ernst Lubitsch's *Sumurun* (1920) and Fritz Lang's *Destiny* (1921). Aladdin's most significant appearance in these years was in German filmmaker Lotte Reiniger's full-length animated film *The Adventures of Prince Achmed* (1926), which devoted one of the film's five acts to his backstory. The emerging Indian film industry was similarly enthralled by "Aladdin" and other stories from the *Nights* in these early years of cinema, even before the success of American imports like *The Thief of Bagdad* consolidated the genre. Disney's animated feature is only one late installment in a long tradition of portraying "Aladdin" on the big screen.

As the story of Aladdin and his magical lamp cycled through European translations and adaptations, it was integrated into the basic vocabulary of Western letters. In some cases, authors merely deployed Aladdin as a familiar reference point in tales of exotic adventure. In *The Count of Monte Cristo*, for instance, Alexandre Dumas stages an *Arabian Nights* fantasy in a Mediterranean setting that features a cave of treasures presided over by Sindbad the Sailor and an Aladdin character drawn to the fantastic visions induced by hashish. The darker side of the dreamworld offered by Aladdin's lamp is also highlighted in Robert Louis Stevenson's short story "The Bottle Imp," where the protagonist buys a bottle that grants wishes, but must contend with the risk of eternal damnation if he dies with the magic bottle in his possession. In Stevenson's version of the fairy tale, nothing is free.

Despite the story's obvious association with supernatural interventions and alternate realities, authors operating in a realist mode have also deployed Aladdin's lamp as a metaphor for dreams of freedom and prosperity—even when they seem liable to collapse. In *Moby-Dick*, Aladdin's lamp symbolizes the special pleasures generated by the successful pursuit of the precious resource of whale oil. While the ordinary merchantman must "dress in the dark, and eat in the dark, and stumble in darkness to his pallet," the whaleman "lives in light. He makes his berth an Aladdin's lamp, and lays him down in it; so that in the pitchiest night the ship's black hull still houses an illumination." For Dickens, who immersed himself in the storytelling devices of the *Arabian Nights*, the story of Aladdin provided a template for thinking about the play of fate within the complex landscape of the Victorian city. Characters such as Dick Swiveller in *The Old Curiosity Shop* seem to benefit from their own mysterious jinn—falling into an *Arabian Nights* dream where marriage to "the Princess of China" is accompanied by the summoning of "black slaves with jars of jewels on their heads." A more sustained use of references to "Aladdin" runs through Dickens's essays for *Household*

Words, where the marvels of the hidden cave and the powers of the jinn pale before the vast treasure generated by a certain London firm and the sudden appearance of palaces in the surburban outskirts—the product of forces beyond human understanding.[1]

The power of tales of the *Arabian Nights*—and Aladdin's lamp—to unlock the sense of wonder in childhood dreams forms a consistent thread in the literature of the twentieth century as writers have reflected on their own hybrid cultural inheritance. In his memoir *Aké*, Nobel laureate Wole Soyinka associates the tales of "Aladdin" and "Ali Baba" with biblical stories of miracle and a realm of magic that may be entered through the consumption of the forbidden fruit of childhood. The pomegranate "with its stone-hearted look and feel unlocked the cellars of Ali Baba, extracted the genie from Aladdin's lamp, plucked the strings of the harp that restored David to sanity, parted the waters of the Nile and filled our parsonage with incense from the dim temple of Jerusalem." For Salman Rushdie, retelling "Aladdin" in post-imperial London in *The Satanic Verses* was an opportunity to wrestle with colonial legacies and the frustrated aspirations of youth. In his native Mumbai, the young Saladin yearns for the magic lamp that rests next to the gilded tomes of Burton's edition of the *Thousand and One Nights* in his father's study, only for his stern father to withhold

---

1 See Richard Maxwell, *Mysteries of Paris and London* (Charlottesville: University of Virginia Press, 2015).

the lamp as a metaphor of the freedom he is denied. In the last chapter of the novel, "A Wonderful Lamp," this conflict unexpectedly gives way to the fairy tale of Saladin's reconciliation not only with his ailing father but also with the cosmopolitan heritage of his Muslim Indian upbringing.

Female authors have sometimes invoked "Aladdin" to refer not to boundless freedom and possibilities but to the specific challenges and limitations they face as women and writers. Clarice Lispector used her first encounter with the tale to signal her dissatisfaction with the possibilities open to her as a woman in mid-twentieth century Brazil. Evoking a stand-alone edition of "Aladdin," one of the first books she read, she recalled her early sense that she was unlikely to get what she wanted by wishing but would have to create her own opportunities. The Argentine writer Victoria Ocampo wrote that even if she "could have a magic lamp like Aladdin and, by rubbing it, could have the power to write like Shakespeare, Dante, Goethe, Cervantes, or Dostoevsky," she would not make that wish, for "a woman cannot unburden herself of her thoughts and feelings in a man's style, just as she cannot speak with a man's voice."

The image of Aladdin and his magic lamp is so ubiquitous that the scholar of folklore Ulrich Marzolph has coined the term "Aladdin Syndrome" to refer to the tendency to use this story to represent the *Thousand and One Nights*, Arabic literature, and Middle Eastern cultures as a whole. In popular culture, the telling and retelling of "Aladdin" becomes like a game of telephone, in which representations of Middle Eastern cultures and peoples become increasingly garbled. As the symbolism of "Aladdin" became detached from its original source, it could be deployed with both positive and negative connotations within American popular culture. In the mid-nineteenth century, for instance, as middle-class and upper-class Americans experienced a steady rise in prosperity, Aladdin became a useful metaphor for consumer dreams fueled by capitalist expansion.[2] Most Americans today know "Aladdin" from the 1992 Disney animated film, which often plays up racial stereotypes in the portrayal of characters who appear to be a curious hodgepodge of Middle Eastern cultures. Perhaps the most striking symptom of "Aladdin Syndrome" is the poll of Republican primary voters conducted in December 2015 in which 30 percent of those polled supported the U.S. bombing of Agrabah, the fictional city in which Disney's *Aladdin* takes place.

Despite the story's popularity and influence, "Aladdin" tends to be treated as an afterthought in English translations of the *Arabian Nights*. In the nineteenth century Edward Lane simply omitted the tale, as he believed all the stories added in French were spurious. The pre-Raphaelite poet John Payne only included the tale in a volume appended to

---

2 Susan Nance, *How the Arabian Nights Inspired the American Dream, 1790–1935* (Durham: University of North Carolina Press, 2009). On the broader significance of "Aladdin Syndrome," see Edward Said, *Orientalism* (New York: Pantheon, 1978).

his translation after it appeared in an Arabic manuscript (later confirmed to be a forgery). Richard Burton likewise added the story in a supplemental volume to his *Arabian Nights*—burnishing his reputation for linguistic mastery by claiming that he preferred to work from a South Asian vernacular version rather than the French. Thinking of Burton, Jorge Luis Borges suggested that each weather-worn adventurer who attempted the *Nights* sought to obliterate his predecessor—giving rise to a line of translators defined by the performance of an aggressive literary masculinity. Lost within this narrative is the fact that many of the most widely distributed versions of "Aladdin" and other *Nights* tales were the result of the labor of female editors and illustrators like Mary Elizabeth Braddon and Virginia Frances Sterrett.

Recent translators of the *Thousand and One Nights* from Arabic have been more inclined to follow in Lane's footsteps when approaching "Aladdin." In preparing his English version, Husain Haddawy dismissed the added French tales as the grime that the editor and the translator needed to remove in order to restore the authentic core of the story collection. Haddawy's publisher would later insist that he include "Aladdin" and "Ali Baba" in an additional volume of "popular tales," but these stories are treated as an afterthought. Talented translators from Arabic have not always been as comfortable working from French. The result is that English translations of "Aladdin" have tended to be either dated and overwrought, or on the dry side. All are swamped within larger volumes of stories of varying quality.

The recent discovery of Diyab's memoir and his account of giving the tales to Galland has shown that "Aladdin" is not strictly a French invention, but rather Syrian-French in its origin and composition. In the spirit of this fresh understanding of the story's provenance, it has been a blessing to find a translator at home in both Arabic and French, equally at ease with the *Thousand and One Nights* as with eighteenth century French. A writer herself, a scholar of literature fluent in English, French, and Arabic, and, as fate would have it, of Syrian-French background, Yasmine Seale is uniquely suited to the task. She also reminds us of the importance of reading the story within the frame of the *Thousand and One Nights*, and of excavating the voice of its imperiled female narrator from beneath the men who have shaped and reshaped her. "Galland's text moves at an elegant, almost stately pace," Seale wrote to me as she translated the text, "but I kept thinking about what it would sound like if we were to hear Shahrazad herself. She is quite literally telling this story to save her life. I kept imagining a kind of manic energy running beneath Galland's decorous prose. It is a symphony to be played *prestissimo*."

Great storytellers tend to be great readers. We know from the frame of the *Thousand and One Nights* that Shahrazad is a woman who has studied many books, and knows poetry by heart. As she sits up weaving the tale of Aladdin for the delight of her husband and would-be executioner, she acknowledges her debt to these other voices by referring enigmatically to "the authors of this story." The pages that follow offer a channel, through Galland's telling of "Aladdin," for all those who may have told it before him—not a single voice but a chorus, singing to each other across the years. If we cannot strip away the many layers to find some authentic kernel, we can at least get to the heart of the appeal of the story—the fluid boundary between the real and the uncanny that has provided such fertile ground for the visions of so many artists across the world, who together have kept alive, by ceaselessly reinventing it, this story of a boy and a magical lamp.

—Paulo Lemos Horta

The Story of

Aladdin

or

The Magic Lamp

⌒

AS SHE FINISHED HER STORY, SHAHRAZAD PROMISED THE
SULTAN ANOTHER NO LESS ENCHANTING THE FOLLOWING
DAY. HER SISTER, DUNYAZAD, MADE SURE TO REMIND
HER BEFORE DAYBREAK OF HER PROMISE, AND SAID THE
SULTAN WAS READY TO HEAR HER. SHAHRAZAD DID NOT
KEEP HIM WAITING. THIS IS THE STORY SHE TOLD HIM.

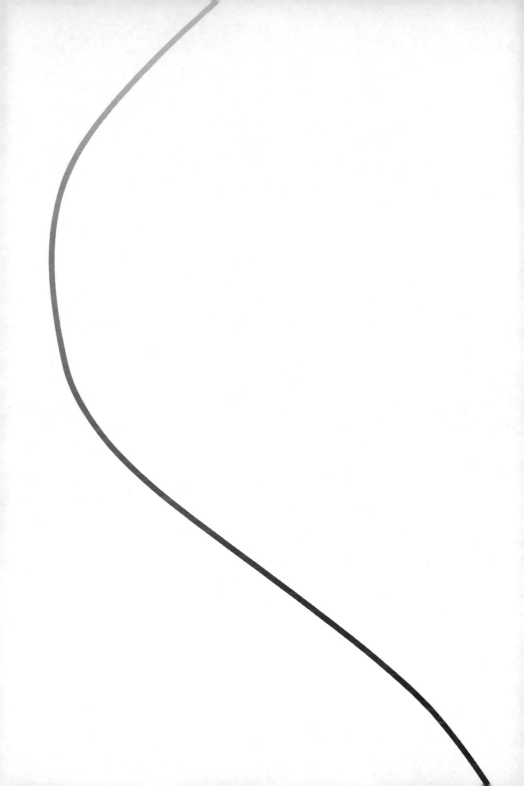

The Tailor's Son

Majesty, in the capital of one of China's vast and wealthy kingdoms, whose name escapes me at present, there lived a tailor named Mustafa, who had no other distinction but his craft. This tailor was very poor, and his work scarcely earned him enough to feed himself, his wife, and a son that God had given them.

The son, whose name was Aladdin, had received a careless upbringing, which instilled in him wild tendencies: he grew to be cruel, stubborn, and rebellious. After a certain age his parents could not keep him indoors, and he spent his days playing in the streets and public squares with idle boys, some even younger than himself.

When Aladdin was old enough to learn a craft, his father, who knew only his own, took him into the shop and tried to teach him needlework. But neither gentleness nor punishment could still his son's wandering mind. As soon as the tailor had his back turned, Aladdin would escape and stay out until evening, and, unable to change his ways, Mustafa was forced to abandon his son to his dissipation. This pained him, and the grief of failing to guide his son to his duty brought about such a violent illness that he died a few months later.

Aladdin's mother, seeing her son renounce his father's craft, closed the shop and had all his tools melted into silver, which, together with the little she earned spinning cotton, kept them both alive.

No longer restrained by the fear of his father, and so untroubled by his mother that he turned on her at the slightest rebuke, Aladdin gave in fully to his dissolute ways. He surrounded himself with boys of his own age and threw himself into their games, idling the years away until he was fifteen, without the slightest curiosity for anything at all and with no thought of what he might become. Then one day, while Aladdin was playing in a square with his band of vagabonds, a stranger passing by stopped to look at him.

This stranger was a remarkable sorcerer, whom the authors of this story have called the Maghrebi magician, and that is what I shall call him, since he was indeed from North Africa, and had arrived only two days before.

Whether or not the magician, who knew the art of reading faces, had seen in Aladdin's features the answer to his journey's quest, he inquired discreetly about his family, his condition, and his character. When he had learned all he wished to know, he approached the young man and steered him a little way from his friends.

"My boy," he said, "isn't your father Mustafa the tailor?"

"He was," replied Aladdin, "but he has been dead a long time."

At these words, the magician threw his arms around Aladdin and kissed him many times, sighing and full of tears. Aladdin asked him why he wept.

"Ah, my boy," cried the magician, "how could I not? I am your uncle, and your father was my dear brother. My travels have kept me away for many years, and just as I return in the hope of seeing him again and giving him the pleasure of my homecoming, you tell me he is dead. It aches to be deprived of that consolation. But I see his face in yours, and that, at least, is some comfort."

Reaching for his purse, he asked Aladdin where his mother lived, and when the answer came, the magician handed him a pocketful of change.

"Go to your mother," he said, "give her my compliments, and say that if time permits I will visit her tomorrow, so that I may see the house where my dear brother lived and died."

When the magician took his leave of the nephew he had

just invented, Aladdin ran to his mother's house, pleased with his pocketful of coins.

"Mother," he said, "do I have any uncles?"

"None," replied his mother, "neither on your father's side nor on mine."

"And yet I have just seen a man who claims to be my father's brother. He even set about kissing me, weeping, when I told him my father was dead. If you don't believe me, look at what he gave me. He sends you his compliments, and said he would come and greet you in person tomorrow, to see the house where my father lived and died."

"It is true," said his mother, "that your father had a brother, but he died a long time ago, and I never heard him mention another."

The following day, the magician approached Aladdin a second time, as he was playing in another part of town with other children. Again he embraced him, and, handing him two gold coins, he said: "Take these to your mother, and tell her to expect me for supper this evening. But first, tell me where the house is." He told him, and the magician let him go.

Aladdin brought the gold coins home to his mother. She spent the money on provisions and the day preparing supper, and, as she lacked much of the tableware she would need, she went to borrow some from the neighbors. When it was ready she said to Aladdin: "Your uncle may not know how to find us. Go out and lead him here if you see him." He was ready to leave when there was a knock at the door.

He opened it and the magician entered, laden with wine and fruit. These he gave to Aladdin, and, after greeting his mother, he asked her to show him the place on the sofa where Mustafa used to sit. She showed him, and he fell upon the spot with kisses and tears.

"My poor brother!" he cried. "How sad I am to have come too late to embrace you once more before you left us!" Though Aladdin's mother offered, he could not bring himself to sit in the same place. "I would not dare," he said, "but allow me to sit across from it, here, and imagine his presence among us." Aladdin's mother did not insist and let him sit where he pleased.

When the magician had chosen his seat, he spoke.

"My dear sister," he began, "do not be surprised that this is our first meeting: it has been forty years since I left this country, which is mine no less than it was my late brother's. In that time, I have traveled to India, to Persia, to Arabia, to Syria, and to Egypt, and stayed in their finest cities, before moving on to the Maghreb, where I settled. In the end, since it is natural, however far one strays from the land of one's birth, never to let its memory fade, I formed such a strong desire to see my country again and to embrace my dear brother, while I still had the strength to undertake the journey, that I made my preparations and set off without delay. I will say nothing of the time it has taken me, nor of all the obstacles I met and the trouble I suffered to arrive here. I will only tell you that nothing has caused me more distress on my travels than the news of my brother's death.

I recognized his features in my nephew's face, and that is how I picked him out from the other children. He will have told you how I received the dreadful news, but we must praise God for all things. I am comforted, at least, to see his face in that of his son."

The magician, seeing the mother falter at the memory of her husband, changed the subject, and, turning to Aladdin, asked him for his name.

"My name is Aladdin."

"Well, Aladdin, how do you occupy yourself? Do you have a craft?"

Unsettled by the question, Aladdin averted his eyes. His mother answered instead.

"Aladdin is lazy," she said. "His father did all he could to teach him his trade and got nowhere. Since he died, despite all my efforts, my son's only occupation has been to roam the streets where you found him, playing with the other children, though he is no longer a child. Unless you can talk some shame into him, I despair of what he will become. He knows that his father had nothing to his name, and that for all my spinning I struggle to feed us both. One day I will show him the door and send him out into the world alone."

At these words Aladdin's mother began to weep. "This is no good, my boy," said the magician. "You must think of earning your keep. There are all kinds of trades, and you are bound to find one you like more than the others. Perhaps what suited your father is not right for you. There is no need to hide anything from me: I only want to help." As

Aladdin said nothing, he went on. "If you are reluctant to learn a craft and wish to become a gentleman, I can set you up as a cloth merchant. You would have your own shop, and you would make an honorable living. Consider it, and tell me frankly what you think. You will always find me ready to keep my promise."

The offer flattered Aladdin, who disliked manual work, and who was not such a fool that he did not know that the shops in question were clean and sought-after, and their merchants well dressed and well respected. He declared to the magician, whom he now regarded as his uncle, that he felt more drawn to the cloth trade than to any other, and that he would always be indebted to him for his kindness. "Since you like the idea," said the magician, "I will take you with me tomorrow and have you dressed in splendid new clothes worthy of the richest merchants in this city. The following day we shall set you up in your shop."

Aladdin's mother, who until then had not believed that the magician might be her husband's brother, banished all doubt after hearing what he pledged to do for her son. She thanked him for his good intentions and, after urging Aladdin to show himself worthy of all the blessings his uncle had promised, served supper. Their talk ran on the same subject all through the meal, until the magician, who saw that it was late, took leave of the mother and her son.

The next morning he returned as promised, and took Aladdin off with him to a merchant who sold clothes made from the finest fabrics and cut for every age and circumstance. He asked for Aladdin's size, and, after setting aside the most beautiful items and discarding the others, told him to take his pick. Charmed by his new uncle's generosity, Aladdin chose an outfit, and the magician paid for it without haggling.

When Aladdin saw himself so magnificently dressed from head to toe, he thanked his uncle in every way he knew, and the magician repeated his promise never to abandon him. He took him to the most fashionable parts of the city, where the shops of rich merchants were, and when they came to the street with the grandest shops selling the very finest cloth, he said to Aladdin: "As you will soon be a merchant like these, you should acquaint yourself with them, and they with you." Then he took him to the most impressive mosques, to the khans where the foreign merchants lodged, and to those parts of the sultan's palace that they had liberty to enter. At last, having seen their fill of the city, they came to the khan where the magician had taken a room. They were met by a party of merchants he had befriended since he arrived, and whom he had invited to dinner in order to introduce them to his so-called nephew.

The feast went on until evening. At length Aladdin made his excuses, and the magician insisted on walking him to his mother's door. When she saw her son in his new clothes, she let out a cry of rapture and a thousand blessings on the magician.

"Dear brother!" she said. "I know that my son does not deserve your gifts, and that he would be unworthy of them if he did not rise to the confidence you have placed in him. As for me, let me thank you again with all my soul, and wish you a life long enough to be a witness to his gratitude, for which he could find no better expression than to govern himself as you have proposed."

"Aladdin is a good boy," the magician replied. "He listens to me, and I believe we will make something of him. My only worry is that I cannot fulfill what I promised to do tomorrow, as it is Friday and the shops will be closed, and we cannot hope to rent and furnish one of our own while the other merchants have a mind only for leisure. We will put off our business to Saturday, but let us still keep our appointment tomorrow. I will take him to the gardens where the fashionable crowd likes to be seen. I do not think he knows much of the entertainments they enjoy there. He has tasted so far only childish pleasures. Now he must see those of men." Then the magician went on his way. Aladdin, elated by his new clothes, was now thrilled at the thought of seeing the gardens outside the city, for he had never left its walls, nor glimpsed its surroundings.

A Ring and a Lamp

Aladdin rose and dressed early the next morning so he would be ready when his uncle came to fetch him. After he waited for what seemed a long time, impatience sent him to the door. He stood on the threshold, hoping to see his uncle arrive, and when he spotted the magician he called goodbye to his mother and ran to meet him.

The magician was full of tenderness for Aladdin. "Let us go, my boy," he said with a smile. "I want to show you some wonderful things." They passed through a gate which led to a series of splendid houses, or rather palaces, each with magnificent gardens that could be freely entered.

Before each palace they passed, the magician asked Aladdin whether he found it beautiful, and Aladdin, seeing the next one loom into view, would answer ahead of the question: "Uncle, that palace is even lovelier than all those we have seen." Still they pressed on into the countryside, and the wily magician, who wanted to go even further to carry out his design, stepped inside one of the gardens. He went to sit by a large fountain, which the nostrils of a bronze lion supplied with fresh water, and feigned exhaustion. "You must be just as tired as I am," he said to Aladdin. "Let us catch our breath here. We shall need all our strength for the rest of our walk."

While they were sitting there, the magician unfolded a handkerchief that hung from his belt, where he had concealed all sorts of cakes and fruits, and which he spread out on the edge of the fountain. He shared a cake with Aladdin and let him choose from the fruit. As they ate, he advised the boy to part ways with his childish friends and instead to seek the company of wise and cautious men. "Soon," he said, "you will be a man like them, and it is never too early to learn from their example." When they had finished their meal, they got up and proceeded through the gardens, which were set apart from each other only by the slim furrows that marked their borders without impeding access; such was the good faith of the city's inhabitants that they needed no other boundaries to protect themselves from trouble. By degrees the magician led Aladdin out of the gardens and into the countryside, until they had almost reached the mountains.

Aladdin, who had not walked so far in his life, was weary.

"Uncle," he said, "where are we going? We have left the gardens far behind us, and all I see now are mountains. If we walk any farther, I am afraid I would not have the strength to go back to the city."

"Take courage, my boy," said the false uncle, "I want to show you another garden, which outshines all those you have seen. It is only a few paces from here. When we arrive, you will tell me yourself what a shame it would have been to have missed it, having come so close."

Aladdin yielded, and the magician took him much farther still, beguiling him all the while with stories.

At last they reached a narrow pass between two mountains. It was to this strange place that the magician had sought to lure Aladdin; now he could realize the dream that had brought him from the edge of Africa all the way to China. "We will go no farther," said the magician. "I want to show you rare and wonderful things. But first, gather up the driest brushwood you can find while I kindle a fire."

The undergrowth was so dense that Aladdin had soon collected enough in the time the magician took to light a flame. As the wood burned, the magician scattered a few drops of fragrant oil over the fire. A thick column of smoke rose up, which he swayed this way and that with a sweep of his hand, muttering words Aladdin did not understand.

At that moment the earth trembled and cracked, revealing beneath its surface a stone, about a foot square, laid flat and fitted with a bronze ring by which it could be lifted. Aladdin, terrified, tried to flee, but the magician detained him, and in his anger struck him so hard across the cheek that he fell to earth. There flowed from him such a quantity of blood it seemed that his front teeth had been knocked clean out of his mouth.

"Uncle!" poor Aladdin cried, trembling and tearful, "what have I done to deserve your blows?"

"I have my reasons," replied the magician. "I am your uncle; I may as well be your father. You are not to talk back to me. But fear nothing," he said more softly. "All I ask is your obedience, if you are to be worthy of the great reward that will soon be yours to enjoy."

These promises appeared to ease Aladdin's fears. When the magician saw that he had regained his trust, he went on.

"Beneath this stone is a treasure destined for you, which will make you richer than the greatest kings of the earth. No one but you is allowed to touch the treasure; even I am forbidden from going near it. But to find it you must do exactly as I say."

At the thought of the treasure, Aladdin forgot his fears. "I will obey," he said. "What should I do?"

"Take that ring," said the magician, "and lift up the stone."

"But I am not strong enough," said Aladdin, "I need your help."

"You do not need anyone. Besides, nothing would happen

if I helped you. You must lift it alone. Say the names of your father and grandfather when you take hold of it, and you will find it no weight at all."

Aladdin did as the magician said and lifted the stone with ease.

The space beneath revealed a set of steps leading into a vault three or four feet deep.

"Go down," said the magician. "At the foot of those steps is an open door leading into three large rooms. There you will find many bronze vessels full of gold and silver, but you must go through the rooms without touching anything. Not even your cloak must brush the walls; keep it wrapped close around you. Otherwise you would die in an instant. The third room will lead you into a garden of fine trees heavy with fruit. Walk on until you see a flight of fifty steps. At the top is an alcove, and in the alcove, a lamp. Take the lamp, throw out the oil it contains, and bring it to me. Do not worry about staining your cloak: the fuel is not really oil, and the lamp will be dry as soon as you have poured it out. As for the fruits in the garden, you may pick as many as you wish. That is not forbidden."

He slipped a ring off his finger and gave it to Aladdin, saying it would protect him from harm. "Go now," he said, "and be brave. We shall both be rich for the rest of our lives."

Aladdin went into the vault and passed through the rooms with great caution, afraid of death. He crossed

the garden like the wind, flew up the stairs, took the
burning lamp from its niche, threw out the wick with
the oil, and, finding it as dry as the magician had said,
put it in his cloak. Back down the steps he went, paus-
ing only to consider the trees, which were bright with
extraordinary fruit: there were white fruits, others clear
and smooth as crystal, and red fruits, some darker than
others, and also green, blue, violet, and yellowish fruits,
and other colors too. Looking closer, Aladdin saw that
the white ones were pearls; the clear and smooth ones,
diamonds; the red were rubies, some darker than others; the green, emeralds; the blue, turquoise; the violet, amethysts; the yellowish ones were sapphires, and
so it was with the others, all of them jewels. Their size
was unimaginable and their beauty without description.
Aladdin, who had no idea of their value, was not struck
by the sight of these fruits, and was not drawn to them as
he might have been to figs or grapes, or any of the other
fine fruits that grow in China. Nor was he old enough
to know their worth: he thought them nothing more
than colored glass. And yet he was compelled, by their
beauty and size, and by the variety of their colors, to
pick them from the trees. He filled both his pockets with
these fruits, as well as the two new pouches which the
magician had bought with his clothes, and even wrapped
some in the fabric of his belt, which was a long bolt of
silk, to keep them from falling.

Unaware of the riches he carried, Aladdin hurried back

through the rooms with the same caution as before and arrived at the mouth of the vault, where the magician stood ready to meet him.

"Please," said Aladdin, "give me your hand and help me up."

"First give me the lamp," said the magician. "It might weigh you down."

"Forgive me," replied Aladdin, "it is no weight at all. I will hand it to you as soon as I am out."

The magician insisted on having the lamp first, but Aladdin, who had buried it beneath the piles of fruit he carried, refused. The magician went into a dreadful rage, and, throwing some of his oil on the fire, he spoke a few magic words, and the stone rolled back over the vault, and the earth closed over the stone.

C⌒

NOW, THIS MAGICIAN was not, as he had claimed, the brother of Mustafa the tailor. It follows that he was no uncle of Aladdin's either. He was, in fact, from North Africa, where he had been born, and since the Maghreb is a place more given to magic than any other, he had applied himself to it since childhood. After forty years of spells and study, of divination by sand and by smoke, he had discovered the existence of a magic lamp, which would make him more powerful than any ruler in the universe if he could only become its owner. His last geomantic reading had revealed to him that the lamp was buried underground in the middle of China. Certain of this revelation, he had left the edge of Africa, and after an arduous journey had arrived in the town that lay closest to the treasure.

And yet, though he had discovered the lamp's location, it was not permitted to him to remove it, nor to enter the underground chamber himself. Another had to go in his place, find the lamp, and bring it back to him. For this purpose he had picked out Aladdin, who seemed to him a boy of no consequence, and determined, once he had the lamp in his hands, to perform the sorcery I have described and sacrifice the poor fool to his greed, so that there should be no witnesses. By striking him on the face and imposing his will, he sought only to encourage in Aladdin a habit of fear and submission, so that when the magician came to ask for the lamp, Aladdin would hand it over at once. But the opposite ensued. In the end he betrayed Aladdin sooner than he had intended, fearing that if they argued any longer, someone might overhear them and make known what he had tried to conceal.

When the magician saw his great hopes dashed, he had no choice but to return to his homeland, which he did the very same day. He took a circuitous path to avoid the city he had left with Aladdin, fearing that he would be seen returning without the boy.

That should have been the last anyone heard of Aladdin. But the man who believed he had erased him from the earth had also supplied him with a means of escape. Indeed, the ring was to be Aladdin's salvation, and it is a wonder that its loss, along with that of the lamp, did not drive the magician to despair. Yet magicians are so accustomed to setbacks and disappointments that they never give up on their lifelong diet of dreams, smoke, and visions.

The Slave of the Ring

When Aladdin found himself buried alive, he called out to his uncle a thousand times, promising to give him the lamp, but he could no longer be heard, and there he remained in darkness. At last, after giving some release to his tears, he went down to the bottom of the vault to seek light from the garden he had just crossed, but the door leading to it, which had opened by magic, had now been conjured shut. He groped ahead of him, right and left, but the door was gone, and his tears returned as he sat on the step, and he lost hope of ever seeing the light again. Soon, he thought, he would slip from this darkness into the shadows of death.

Aladdin spent two days in this state, without eating or drinking. On the third day, as he considered his inevitable death, he submitted to God, and, joining his hands in prayer, he said: "There is no might and no power except with God!"

As he held his hands together, he inadvertently rubbed the ring which the magician had slipped onto his finger and whose power he still did not know. At that moment an enormous jinni with fearsome eyes rose up from the earth until it filled the vault, and said these words to Aladdin: "What is your command? I am here to obey you as your slave, and the slave of all those who wear the ring, I and the other slaves of the ring."

Aladdin might have been struck silent by such a vision, but now, concerned only with the danger he was in, he replied without hesitation: "Whoever you are, get me out of this place, if such is your power." At once the earth parted and he found himself outside, precisely at the spot where the magician had led him. Aladdin, who had spent so long in the darkest gloom, struggled at first to face the light of day. When his eyes adapted to the glare, he was amazed to see no opening in the earth and could not understand how he had been so swiftly ejected from its bowels. Only by the traces of burnt brushwood could he mark the spot where the vault had been.

Turning toward the city, he caught sight of it among

its outlying gardens, found the path they had walked, and followed it back, thanking God all the while for returning him to the world he thought he had left for good. He reached the city and staggered home, but the joy of seeing his mother again conspired with the effects of his fast, and he fainted. His mother, who had already wept over his death, did all she could to revive him. When at last he came around, he said he had been hungry for three days, and his mother brought him what she had, warning him not to eat too fast in case he harmed himself.

Aladdin followed his mother's advice: he ate slowly and drank in proportion, and when he finished, he said: "Mother, I could take you to task for abandoning me so easily to the mercy of a man who wanted to destroy me, and who is so sure of his success that as I speak to you now, he must be convinced that I have either lost my life or will lose it by morning. But you believed he was my uncle, and I had no reason to doubt it. What else were we to think of a man who covered me in gifts and promises? Yet you must know, Mother, that he is nothing but a traitor and a wretch. His favors were only a means to get rid of me without exciting our suspicion. I can assure you that nothing I did gave him the slightest reason to mistreat me. You will be of the same opinion when I tell you all that I have suffered since we parted."

Aladdin began to relate to his mother what had happened since Friday, when the magician had taken him to see the palaces and gardens outside the city, and all that took place on the way, until they reached the point between the mountains where the magician was to carry out his deed; how, with a little oil on the fire and a muttered spell, the earth had parted to reveal a vault, which led down to a fathomless treasure. He made sure to mention the blow he had received from the magician, who, having softened a little, had lured him, with promises and the ring on his finger, into the vault. He was careful to report everything he had seen as he crossed and recrossed the three rooms, the garden, and the alcove where he had found the magic lamp.

He showed her the lamp and the fruits he had gathered in the garden. These fruits were precious stones, which shone like the sun even in the bright room, but Aladdin's mother knew no more about such things than her son. She had grown up in poverty and had never had any jewels, nor seen them worn by friends, so it is no wonder that she saw little use in them, besides the pleasure they gave the eye with their many colors.

Aladdin completed his story by relating how, when he returned to the mouth of the vault, ready to step out of it, as he refused to give his uncle the lamp he wanted, the vault had closed over in an instant by the power of the oil the magician had thrown on the fire, which he had been careful to keep alive, and of the words he had spoken. But Aladdin could not go on without faltering: in tears he described the misery he suffered from the moment he found himself buried alive until he was returned to the world thanks to his ring. "You know the rest," he said. "Such were my adventures, and the dangers I faced since you saw me last."

Aladdin's mother sat patiently through his astonishing story without interrupting. At those moments, however, where the magician's treachery was most apparent, she could not help but give voice to her outrage, and as soon as Aladdin had finished, she flung a thousand curses on the impostor, calling him a traitor, a wretch, a barbarian, a murderer, a cheat, a sorcerer, and an enemy of the human race.

"Yes, my son, a sorcerer. They traffic in spells, the devil's trade. Praise be to God, who did not let the magician's wickedness get the better of you! You must thank Him well for that grace. You would not be alive today had you not remembered Him and begged for His help." She said many more things, never straying far from the hatred she bore for the magician, but as she spoke, she noticed that Aladdin, who had not slept in three nights, needed to rest.

She put him to bed, and retired herself soon after.

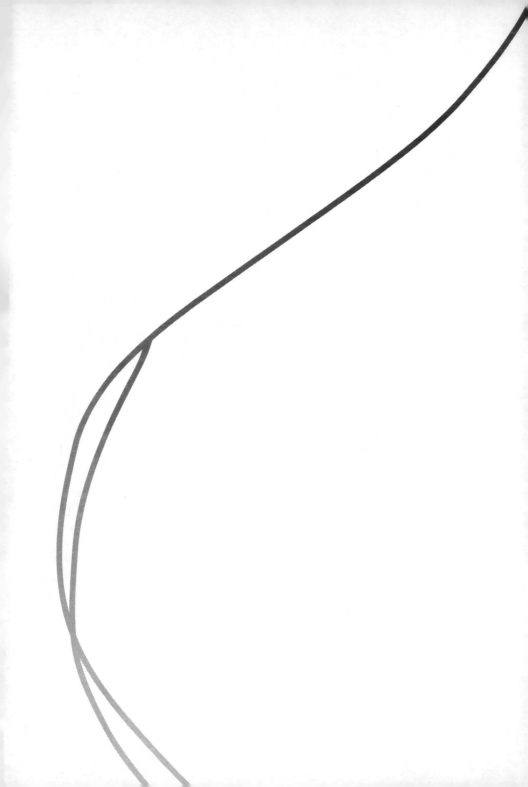

The Slave of the Lamp

Aladdin, who had not rested a moment in his underground prison, spent the night in a deep sleep and did not rise until late. When he woke, he asked to eat.

"Alas," said his mother, "I have not even a piece of bread to give you. But I have a little cotton thread left over, which I will sell to buy bread and something for our dinner."

"Save your cotton," replied Aladdin, "and give me the lamp I brought yesterday. I'll sell it instead. It will provide us with breakfast and lunch, and perhaps supper too."

Aladdin's mother fetched the lamp. As it was very dirty, she took some water and a little sand to clean it with, but hardly had she begun to rub it when a jinni, hideous and gigantic, appeared before her and roared: "What is your command? I am here to obey you as your slave, and the slave of all those who have the lamp, I and the other slaves of the lamp."

Aladdin's mother was in no state to reply. She fainted at the first sight of the jinni, but Aladdin did not wait to act. He seized the lamp, and, speaking for his mother, he said: "I am hungry. Fetch me something to eat!" The jinni returned in an instant bearing a large silver tray on his head, on which rested twelve silver dishes containing fine meats, six white loaves of bread, and two bottles of exquisite wine. In his hands he held two silver cups. He laid everything down on the sofa and disappeared.

When Aladdin's mother came to her senses, she was amazed at the feast laid before her. "Who have we to thank for this abundance?" she asked. "Could it be that the sultan has heard tell of our poverty, and has had mercy on us?" "Mother," replied Aladdin, "let us eat." During their meal, Aladdin's mother never tired of admiring the tray and its dishes, though she could not be sure if they were made of silver or some other material. In truth, since she was unaware of their value, it was only their novelty that held her admiration, nor did her son know any better.

It was noon when they sat down to their meal, and they did not rise before evening. They decided that since the dishes were hot, they may as well combine breakfast, lunch, and dinner, all in a single sitting. When they had finished their extended meal, Aladdin told his mother about the jinni. "In all my years on earth," she said, "I have never heard of anyone seeing one. How could this spirit have appeared to me, though he had appeared to you in the vault?"

"Your jinni," said Aladdin, "is not the same as the one who appeared to me. They are alike in size, but their manner and dress are entirely different: indeed, they belong to different masters. If you remember, the one I saw called himself the slave of the ring I have on my finger, while yours said he was the slave of the lamp. But I do not believe you heard him: you fainted as soon as he began to speak."

"Do you mean to say," she said, "that your lamp is to blame for the jinni? Remove it from my sight; I want nothing to do with it. I beg you to sell the ring too. It is forbidden to deal with the jinn: they are demons. Our prophet said so."

"After all the lamp has given us," replied Aladdin, "I would not sell it just yet. My wicked uncle desired this lamp more than all the gold and silver which he knew to be in those rooms. He knew its power well enough to want nothing more from that vault. Since chance has made us aware of its virtues, let us use it, but discreetly, lest we attract the envy of our neighbors. As for the ring, allow me to keep it and have it always on my finger. Without it, you would not have seen me again. Who knows when some other danger might strike, and I would need its deliverance?" His mother could hardly object, and let him do as he pleased.

The following night after supper, nothing remained of the good food the jinni had brought. In the morning, before hunger could bite, Aladdin took one of the silver dishes under his cloak and went out to sell it. On the way he met a Jewish merchant, to whom he showed the dish and asked if he wanted to buy it. The merchant, recognizing it as good silver, asked him how much it was worth. Aladdin, who had no idea, and who had never traded in such goods, simply said he was well aware of the dish's value and would count on the man's good faith. Put out by his ingenuity, the merchant took from his purse a gold coin which made up at most one seventy-second of the dish's value, and presented it to him. Aladdin seized the coin, and ran away so quickly that the merchant, not content with the profit he had just made, cursed himself for not having realized that Aladdin knew nothing of the price of his dish, and that he might have given him much less. He thought of running after the young man to try and win back some of his money, but Aladdin was racing, and was already too far to reach.

They lived on the coin for a few days, and when money ran out, Aladdin sold another dish to the merchant, until he had sold all twelve. The merchant, who had paid a gold coin for the first, did not dare offer less for the others, for fear of losing out on the bargain. When nothing remained of the silver dishes, Aladdin went for the tray, which alone weighed ten times more than any single dish. He wanted to take it to another merchant, but the weight of it stopped him and he was obliged once again to seek out the same merchant, who paid him ten gold coins.

While the ten gold coins lasted, they were spent on the needs of the household. Aladdin, who was used to an idle life, had renounced the company of other boys since his adventure with the magician. Now he spent his days walking or in conversation with people he met. Sometimes he stopped in the merchants' shops, where he liked to listen in on the discussions, which over time gave him some understanding of the world.

When nothing remained of the ten gold coins, Aladdin turned to the lamp, and the jinni brought them another feast. After the meal there remained enough for them to live well for two more days.

When they were out of food and money, Aladdin took a silver dish and went to find the merchant to sell it to him. On his way, he passed the shop of an old silversmith who was known for his honesty. The silversmith spotted him and called him in. "My son," he said, "I have seen you pass by many times, always carrying something as you are now, always going to meet the same merchant, and always returning empty-handed. No doubt you have been selling him your wares. But you are perhaps unaware that this merchant is a cheat, and that none of those who know him will trade with him. If you wished to show me what you are selling, I would faithfully pay you its full price."

Aladdin pulled the dish from his cloak. The old man,

who saw that it was made of fine silver, asked him if he had sold any other dishes to the merchant, and how much the merchant had paid for them. Aladdin confessed that he had sold twelve, and that the merchant had only given him a gold coin apiece. "Ah, the thief!" cried the silversmith. "There is no use regretting it. But when you learn the value of your dish, you will see how the merchant has cheated you."

The silversmith took the scales and weighed the dish, and told him that it was worth seventy-two gold coins, which he counted out for him at once. "This," he said, "is the true price of your dish. If you do not believe me, you may ask any one of our silversmiths, and if he tells you it is worth more, I will double my payment."

Aladdin thanked the silversmith warmly, and from then on went only to him when it came to selling the other dishes, for which he always received a fair price. Though the lamp provided Aladdin and his mother with inexhaustible funds, they lived as frugally as before, and continued in this way for many years.

Aladdin, meanwhile, finished his education by visiting the shops of the finest merchants and joining in their conversations, and gradually took on all the manners of fashionable society. From the company of jewelers he learned that the fruits he had picked in the orchard, which he had believed to be colored glass, were in fact immensely precious stones. By observing the sale and purchase of such stones in the shops, he learned something of their worth, and, as he saw none that compared to his own, neither in beauty nor in size, he understood that he was in possession of an incalculable fortune. He had the prudence to tell no one about it, not even his mother, and there is no doubt that his silence was to thank for the great riches he was to acquire.

The Sultan's Daughter

One day, as he strolled through the city, Aladdin heard an order from the sultan proclaiming that all shops and houses were to be locked, and that everyone was to stay indoors until Princess Badr al-Budur, or Moon of Moons, the sultan's daughter, had gone to the baths and returned. Aladdin was seized by a desire to see her face, but he could not peek through the screen of one of the houses near the baths, as he knew the princess would be veiled. Instead he hid himself behind the bathhouse door. Through a slit in the door he saw her arrive, surrounded by a crowd of women and eunuchs. When she was three or four paces from the bathhouse door, she removed her veil.

Until that moment, Aladdin had never seen a woman uncovered except his mother, who was aged now, and whose ordinary features had never led Aladdin to suspect that other women might look any different. He might have heard others talk about beautiful women, but whatever words one might use to describe it, none have the effect of beauty itself.

When Aladdin saw Princess Badr al-Budur, he quickly shed his notion that all women must look more or less like his mother. The princess was the most beautiful woman he had ever seen: she had brown hair, large, bright eyes, a soft and modest gaze, a flawless nose, a small mouth, lovely crimson lips, and all her features were in symphony. Aladdin reeled, shocked by such a combination of marvels. She was tall too, and carried herself magnificently, which drew the respect of all who saw her.

The princess passed into the bathhouse, and Aladdin stood there for a while in a kind of rapture, retracing and impressing on his memory the figure that had charmed his heart. At last he recovered his senses, and, considering that it would be vain to wait for the princess's exit from the baths, since she would have her back to him and her face covered, he gave up the prospect and went home.

Aladdin could not hide his agitation from his mother.

She asked if he was unwell, but Aladdin said nothing and fell sprawled on the sofa, where he remained, busy only with retracing the lovely image of the princess in his mind. His mother, who was busy with supper, pressed him no further. When the meal was ready, she served it beside him on the sofa and sat down at the table, but, seeing that her son paid no attention to it, she told him to eat, and it was only with the greatest strain that he sat up. He ate much less than usual, his gaze lowered, and withdrew so deeply into himself that his mother could not draw a single word from him. After supper she renewed her questions, but Aladdin preferred to go to bed rather than give his mother any satisfaction on the subject.

Setting aside how Aladdin, overpowered by the beauty of the princess, spent the night, let us simply remark that the following day, as he sat on the sofa facing his mother, who was spinning cotton as usual, he said: "Mother, I will break the silence I have kept since my return from the city yesterday, which I know has wounded you. I was not ill, as you seemed to believe, nor am I now. Yet I could not tell you what I feel. It is worse than a sickness. Its nature is obscure to me, but perhaps you will understand it by what I am about to tell you.

"You may not have heard," he went on, "that yesterday it was announced that Princess Badr al-Budur, the sultan's daughter, would go to the baths after dinner. I learned the news on my walk around the city. An order was proclaimed to close all the shops and stay indoors, in order to show the princess the respect she was due and let her pass freely through the streets. As I was not far from the baths, the curiosity of seeing her uncovered led me to go and stand behind the bathhouse door, fancying that she might remove her veil as she was about to enter. If you remember the door's position, you can imagine that my scheme would have given me a clear view of her. She did, in fact, remove her veil as she went in, and I had the pleasure of seeing the charming princess. That, Mother, is the reason for the state you saw me in yesterday, and the source of my silence. I love the princess with a force I can hardly express. As my passion burns more brightly with every passing moment, it seems my only satisfaction would be to make her mine. That is why I have resolved to ask the sultan for her hand."

Aladdin's mother had listened carefully enough to her son's story, but at these last words she could not help but burst out laughing. Aladdin wanted to go on, but she cut him short: "My son, what are you thinking? You must have lost your mind to be saying these things."

"I can assure you I have not," replied Aladdin, "in fact I have never thought so clearly. I have foreseen your accusations of madness and extravagance, but none of that can deter me. My mind is made up to ask the sultan for his daughter's hand in marriage."

"I must tell you," said his mother very seriously, "that you are not in your right mind. Even if you wanted to act on this decision, I cannot imagine who you could possibly send to ask the sultan."

"You, of course," said Aladdin without hesitation.

"Me!" cried the mother. "To the sultan! And who are you, that you presume to covet your sultan's daughter? Have you forgotten that you are the son of one of the lesser tailors of this city, and of a mother whose ancestors were scarcely more distinguished? Are you aware that sultans are loath to give away their daughters even to the sons of other sultans?"

"I told you I have foreseen these objections," said Aladdin, "and any more you might raise. Your disapproval cannot sway me. Do not refuse me this favor, unless you would prefer to see me die than to give me life again."

Alarmed to see how stubbornly he clung to an idea so lacking in good sense, his mother tried again.

"I am your mother," she said, "and there is nothing within the bounds of reason that I would not do out of love for you. If we were talking of marrying you to the daughter of one of our neighbors, whose condition was similar to ours, I would devote myself, I would do everything in my power to help you, although you would first have to secure some means of an income or learn a craft. But here you are, heedless of your origins, daring to look above your station, to set your sights on no less a person than the daughter of your sovereign, who has only to say a word to crush you. But your fate is yours alone to decide.

As for what concerns me . . . supposing I had the brazenness to appear before His Majesty with such an extravagant request, to whom would I even introduce myself? Do you suppose that the first person I spoke to would not accuse me of lunacy and chase me out? Supposing even that I encountered no such difficulty in gaining access to the sultan, I know that he is quick to welcome his aggrieved subjects, and to grant them the justice they seek. I also know that, to those who come to him seeking mercy and who show themselves to be worthy of it, he is merciful.

But are you one of those, and do you believe you are worthy of the favor you wish to request? What have you done for your sovereign or for your country? How have you distinguished yourself? If you have done nothing to deserve such a favor, if you are not even worthy of it, on what basis could I ask for it? How could I even open my mouth to put the thought to the sultan? His majestic presence and the brilliance of his court would seal my lips at once, I who trembled before your father whenever I had a favor to ask him.

There is another reason, my son, which has not occurred to you, which is that you cannot appear before your sultan empty-handed. A gift ensures that if the favor is refused, the sultan will at least give you his ear. But what gift can you possibly bring? And even if you were to find something worthy of a moment of your monarch's attention, what proportion would there be between your gift and your request? Think on it, and consider that what you desire is impossible."

Aladdin listened calmly to everything his mother came up with to deter him from his course, and, having considered each point of her rebuke, he said: "I admit, Mother, that it is bold of me to dare to presume as I do. You say it is not customary to appear before the sultan empty-handed, and that I have nothing that might be worthy of him. I must confess you are right about the gift; I had not considered it. But when you say I have nothing to offer him, do you not think that what I brought home after the night of my near-death would make a delightful present for the sultan? The things with which I filled my pouches and my belt are not, as we had supposed, only colored glass: they are extremely precious stones, fit only for great monarchs. I learned of their value in the jewelers' shops, but none of those I saw there were comparable to ours, and yet they sell for immense prices. Whatever their value, I am convinced that the sultan cannot but receive them with pleasure. Go and fetch your porcelain bowl, and let us see the effect of all the colors together."

Aladdin's mother brought the bowl, and her son removed the gems from the pouches and laid them out against the porcelain. Mother and son were dazzled by their shine, for they had never seen them other than by the light of the lamp. It is true that Aladdin had seen them on their trees, gleaming like fruit, but, being a child, he had believed the stones to be no more than playthings, and had taken them with nothing else in mind.

"Mother," said Aladdin, "you can no longer evade going to the sultan on the grounds that you have nothing to bring him. This gift will, I believe, earn you a most favorable welcome." So it was that his mother, both out of tenderness for him and fear that he might give in to some extreme act, overcame her resistance and accepted.

As it was late and the time to go to the palace was past, the matter was put off until morning. Mother and son talked of nothing else for the rest of the day, and Aladdin took care to impress on his mother anything that might strengthen her resolve. But despite all his reasons, she was not persuaded that such a venture could ever succeed; it must be admitted that she had every reason to doubt. "Supposing," she said, "the sultan receives me as favorably as we hope, and listens calmly to my proposal, but after that warm welcome asks me about your fortune and your estate—what do you expect me to tell him?"

"Mother," replied Aladdin, "let us not worry ourselves ahead of time over what may not come to pass. Let us first see what sort of welcome you receive from the sultan, and what sort of answer he gives. If he does happen to ask such questions, I will think of a suitable answer. I trust that the lamp, which has been our lifeline all these years, will not fail me when I most need it."

Before the Sultan

Aladdin and his mother retired for the night, but the violent passion and dreams of endless fortune that filled the son's mind stopped him from sleeping as soundly as he would have liked. He rose before first light, went to wake his mother, and pressed her to dress as fast as she could in order to be at the palace gate when it opened.

Aladdin's mother took the porcelain bowl with its gift of gemstones, wrapped it in a napkin, and carried it to the palace. The grand vizier and the lords of council had just entered when she arrived at the gate. She joined the large crowd of people seeking an audience and walked with them to the divan, or council chamber. It was a splendid room, vast and deep, with a magnificent entrance. She placed herself in front of the sultan. Petitioners were called one after the other, and their matters were discussed, debated, and concluded, until the session was over. Then the sultan rose, dismissed his council, and returned to his apartments, followed by the grand vizier and the other ministers. All those who had gathered to have their matters heard left the room, some satisfied with the outcome of their case, others displeased with the judgment made against them, others still hopeful of being heard at another session.

Aladdin's mother judged that the sultan would not appear again that day and went home. Her son, seeing her return with the gift, hardly dared ask after her journey. His mother, who had never set foot in the sultan's palace and had not the first idea of what took place there, spoke with great innocence.

"I saw the sultan," she said, "and I am sure he saw me too. I was standing right in front of him, and nobody stood between us. But he was preoccupied with all the speakers, and it moved me to see the trouble he took to listen to them. It all lasted so long that I think he got bored, for he stood up unexpectedly and withdrew at once, without having heard the many other people who were waiting to speak. Still, it gave me great pleasure to see him, though I too began to lose patience at having to stand for so long. I will go back tomorrow. Perhaps the sultan will not be so busy."

Enamored as he was, Aladdin could not but accept this

excuse and wait. He was at least satisfied that his mother had made the most difficult leap, which was to hold the sultan's gaze, and hoped that the sight of others speaking in his presence had emboldened her to act when a favorable moment came.

The next morning she returned to the palace, but she found the divan closed and learned that the council only sat every other day. She brought this news to her son, who was forced to renew his patience. She went back six times on the appointed days, and might have returned a hundred times just as uselessly if the sultan, who saw her standing before him at every session, had not noticed her.

One day, the sultan said to his grand vizier: "Some time ago I began to notice a certain woman, who attends every session of the council, always carrying a bundle wrapped in cloth. She stands for the full length of the hearing and is always careful to place herself in front of me. Do you know what she wants?"

The grand vizier, who knew no more than the sultan, felt he ought to say something, and replied: "Your Majesty is aware that women often complain about nothing. This woman has no doubt come to carp about the bad flour she was sold, or some other trivial matter."

The sultan was not satisfied with this answer.

"Call her next time," he said, "and let us hear her."

The vizier's only reply was to kiss his hand and raise it above his head, to indicate that he was prepared to lose his head if he failed to obey.

At the next session Aladdin's mother was called forward. She walked after the usher up to the sultan's throne, and, following the example of the others, she knelt and pressed her forehead to the carpet until the sultan told her to rise. "Good woman," he said, "I have seen you often in this divan, standing before me from beginning to end. What brings you here?"

"King of kings," she said, "before I reveal the reason for my presence before your throne, I beg your pardon for the boldness of the question I have come to ask. It is so unusual that I tremble with shame at the thought of submitting it to my sultan." The sultan sent away all but the grand vizier, and told her she could speak without fear.

Once Aladdin's mother had taken all the precautions that her delicate mission required, she told the sultan how Aladdin had seen Princess Badr al-Budur, how that encounter had roused him to an irresistible passion, how he had confessed his love to her, and how she had done all she could to talk him out of an infatuation "no less insolent to Your Majesty," she said, "than to the princess. But he persisted, and even threatened to commit some desperate act if I did not come and ask Your Majesty for the princess's hand. After a terrible struggle I accepted. Now I beg you to forgive not only myself, but my son Aladdin."

The sultan listened to her with great gentleness, without the slightest sign of outrage or even of derision, and asked what she had in her bundle of cloth. She unwrapped the gift and laid the jewels at the foot of the throne.

One could not describe the sultan's surprise when he saw so many precious stones assembled in that bowl, for they were larger, brighter, more precious, and more perfect than any he had seen before. For a while he was so amazed he could not move. When he recovered his composure, he took the gift from Aladdin's mother's hands and gave a cry of joy: "How beautiful these are! How rich!" After picking up and admiring almost every stone in turn, and noting what distinguished each of them, he turned to his grand vizier and said: "Look at these, and tell me if there is anything more precious on this earth. Is this gift not worthy of my daughter, and should I not give her to whoever values her at such a price?"

These words threw the grand vizier into a strange turmoil. Some time before, the sultan had hinted that he wished to marry his daughter to one of the vizier's sons. Now he feared that the beauty of this gift would change his mind.

"No one can deny," he said, "that this present is worthy of the princess. But I implore Your Majesty to grant me three months before making a decision. I hope that by then my son will be able to offer you a gift even more precious than Aladdin's."

The sultan, convinced that his grand vizier could never find his son a present to match this one, still granted him that grace, and told Aladdin's mother that he consented to the marriage, and that she should return after three months.

Aladdin's mother, who had thought an audience with the

sultan impossible, returned home overjoyed. When Aladdin saw his mother enter, both earlier than usual and with smiling eyes, he asked her if he could live in hope.

"My son," she said, "put an end to your agony. Far from thinking of death, you have every reason to rejoice." She went on to relate how she had been heard before anyone else, the precautions she had taken before putting her offer to the sultan, and the favorable response he had given. She added that, as far as she could judge, the gift had impressed him and moved him to approval. "I did not expect it," she said, "as the grand vizier had whispered something into his ear just before he answered me, and I feared that the vizier would turn him away from his good intentions." Aladdin, elated, resolved himself to patience, and counted the hours and days that kept him from his beloved.

Two months had passed when his mother, going into the city one evening to buy oil, found everyone rejoicing and all the shops illuminated. The streets were thick with palace officials in ceremonial dress, mounted on richly caparisoned horses and surrounded by a multitude of footmen who came and went. She asked her oil merchant what was going on. "Where have you been, my good lady?" he said. "Do you not know that the son of the grand vizier is to marry the princess tonight? She will soon be leaving the baths, and the officials that you see all around will escort her back to the palace for the ceremony."

Aladdin's mother ran home. Her son was unprepared for the terrible news she brought.

"All is lost!" she cried. "You hoped for the sultan's beautiful daughter, but it was not to be."

"How could the sultan have broken his promise?" said Aladdin. "How do you know?"

"Tonight," replied his mother, "the grand vizier's son will marry Princess Badr al-Budur at the palace."

She told him the story, in such detail that it left no room for doubt.

Any other man would have given up hope, but a secret jealousy kept Aladdin from despair. Without a single word against the sultan, the vizier, or his son, he simply said: "Mother, the grand vizier's son will perhaps not be as happy as he expects this evening." He went to his room, took the magic lamp he kept there to hide it from his mother, and rubbed it in the same spot his mother had rubbed it before. At once the jinni appeared before him.

"What is your command?"

"The sultan has broken his promise to me, and is marrying the princess to another. I command you to bring me the bride and groom tonight."

"As you wish, master," said the jinni.

Aladdin went back to his mother, and ate as calmly as usual. After supper, he spoke to her a little about the princess's marriage, as though the matter no longer concerned him. He returned to his room, and, while his mother went to bed, he stayed up waiting for the jinni to do his work.

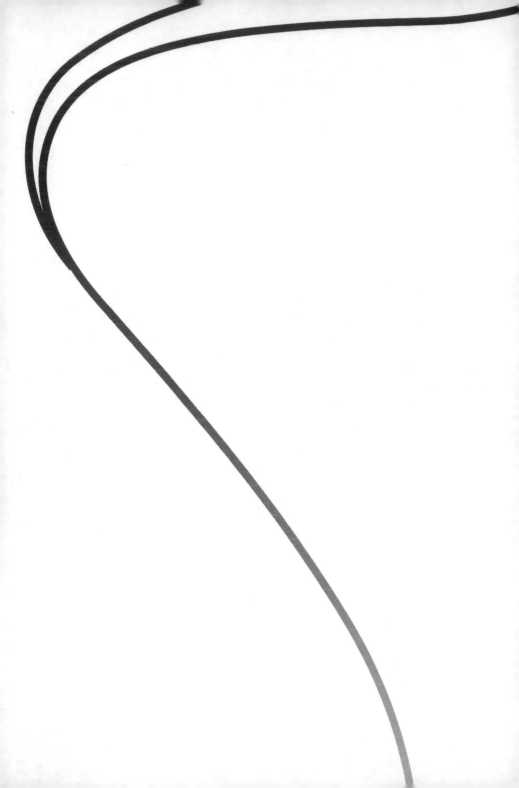

A Wedding Interrupted

Meanwhile, at the palace, the celebrations went on well into the night. At last the grand vizier's son was led into his bride's chamber by the chief eunuch, and went to bed first. Before long the sultana, surrounded by her handmaidens, brought in her daughter. The daughter made a great show of resisting, as is the custom with new brides. The sultana helped her undress, and, after kissing her daughter good night, she withdrew with all her women. The last one to leave closed the door.

No sooner was the door shut than the jinni, before the couple had even had time to embrace, transported them, still in their bed, in an instant to Aladdin's bedroom. "Take this man," said Aladdin to the jinni, "lock him in the out-house, and come back tomorrow at daybreak." The jinni removed the grand vizier's son from the bed in his night-shirt and left him out in the cold, after casting a spell over him to keep him still.

For all his passion, Aladdin did not say much when he found himself alone with the princess. "Have no fear," he said. "You are safe here. If I have been forced to these extreme measures, it was not to offend you, but to prevent an unworthy rival from possessing you, since your father had promised you to me." The princess, who knew nothing of the matter, barely took in these words, and was in no state to reply. The shock of her strange adventure had left her speechless. Aladdin did not stop there: he undressed, and took the place of the grand vizier's son in bed, his back turned to the princess, having placed a sword between them to indicate that he deserved its punishment should he dare to offend her honor.

Delighted to have deprived his rival of the happiness he had flattered himself would be his, Aladdin slept soundly, while the princess passed the most miserable night of her life. Should one remember the state in which the jinni had left the grand vizier's son, one might suppose that his was hardly more restful.

In the morning, Aladdin did not need to rub the lamp to call the jinni. At the appointed hour it appeared, fetched the bridegroom, laid him down by the princess, and returned the bed to the palace. It should be noted that neither the princess nor the grand vizier's son saw the jinni; a glimpse of its hideous form might have killed them. Nor did they hear any of what was said between it and Aladdin. All they perceived was the jolt of hurtling from one place to the next, and this was quite enough to terrify them.

The jinni had just returned the nuptial bed to its place when the sultan entered to wish his daughter good morning. The grand vizier's son, until now still frozen after his long night, jumped up and ran to his dressing room as he heard the door open.

The sultan approached the princess's bed, kissed her between the eyes according to custom, and asked after her night. As he stood back and looked at her more closely, he was astonished to see only a deep melancholy in her eyes, and no other sign that might have set his mind at ease. His daughter would not say a word. As he imagined that she did so out of shyness, he withdrew. Yet he could not help but think there was something strange in her silence, and made straight for the sultana's apartments. "Your Majesty must not be alarmed," she told him. "All brides are shy the day after their wedding. Give her two or three days, then she will receive her father properly. I will go to her now, and would be very much surprised if she gives me the same welcome."

The sultana dressed and went to her daughter, and found her not only speechless but with a look of such dejection that she was alarmed. "Why is it, child, that you hang so limply in my arms? Is it right to treat your mother and father like this? What is the matter?"

At last Princess Badr al-Budur broke the silence with a great sigh.

"Ah, dear Mother," she cried, "forgive me if I have failed to honor you as I must! My mind is haunted by the strange happenings of last night, and my body has not recovered from its shock. I struggle even to recognize myself."

Then she related in the most vivid terms how, the moment she and her groom had laid their heads on the pillow, the bed had been snatched away and transported at once to a dark and dirty room, where she found herself alone without her husband, and where a young man, after saying a few words that fright stopped her from catching, lay down beside her in her husband's place, having put a saber between them, and that in the morning her husband had reappeared and the bed returned to its place in an instant.

"All this had only just happened," she went on, "when my father the sultan entered the room. Such was my stupor and alarm that I could not say a single word. No doubt he is offended by the way I repaid the honor of his visit, but I hope he will forgive me when he learns of my miserable adventure."

The sultana listened calmly to the princess's tale and believed none of it. "You did well to hold your tongue around your father," she said. "Be careful not to mention any of this to others: they would think you mad. Now get up, and shake these dreams from your mind. It would not do for such a fantasy to get in the way of your wedding celebrations. Can you not hear the fanfare already, the trumpets, the cymbals, and the drums? Their music will drive these fancies from your spirit."

The festivities went on all day in the palace. The sultana stood by her daughter and did all she could to buoy her up, yet it was plain to see that her mind was elsewhere. The grand vizier's son was no less preoccupied after his awful night, but ambition drove him to dissemble, and no one doubted that he was a happy husband.

Aladdin had no intention of letting the couple rest, and as soon as night had fallen he turned to the lamp again. "Jinni," he said, "the vizier's son and the princess will sleep together tonight. Go, and when they are in bed, bring them to me as you did yesterday."

The jinni served Aladdin as faithfully as he had the night before, the grand vizier's son was just as cold and uncomfortable as he had been the first time, and the princess was just as mortified to find herself in bed with Aladdin, with only a saber between them. At first light the jinni reappeared and restored them to the palace chamber.

The sultan, anxious to know how she had spent the night, paid his daughter an early visit. The grand vizier's son, even more appalled by this last misadventure than by the first, threw himself into his dressing room as soon as he heard the sultan approach.

The sultan greeted his daughter, and, after his usual embrace, said: "Well, my child, is your temper as foul today as it was yesterday? Will you tell me how you slept?" But again she refused to say a word. Only after he threatened to cut off her head did she speak.

"My dear father and sultan," she pleaded, on the edge of tears, "I hope that you will change anger for compassion once you have heard my account of last night and the night before."

She told him the true story of those two dreadful nights, in such a poignant manner that love and tenderness lanced through him as she spoke. "If you have the slightest doubt about the truth of my tale, ask the husband you have given me if it was not so."

The sultan sat brooding over the anguish such a strange adventure must have brought the princess. "My daughter," he said, "you are very wrong not to have spoken up yesterday about this bizarre affair, which concerns me as much as it does you. I did not marry you to make you miserable, but rather to give you all the happiness one could have expected from a husband who seemed to suit you well. Now shake these awful visions from your spirit. I will see to it that the nights ahead are not so restless as the ones that have passed."

Back in his quarters, the sultan told the grand vizier to find his son. The grand vizier pressed him to set the story straight.

"I cannot hide the truth from you, Father," said the son. "All the princess has said is so. But she cannot have told you about the cruel treatment that was reserved for me. Since my wedding day I have spent two of the most brutal nights it is possible to imagine. I lack the words to describe the particular hell I endured, not to mention the horror of being whisked away by unseen hands no less than four times, without the first idea of how such a thing was possible. You shall form your own judgment of the state I was in, when I tell you that I spent two nights standing naked in my nightshirt in some narrow outhouse, unable to move or change position, though there seemed to be nothing stopping me. Though none of these trials has diminished the love I bear the princess, I would rather die than persist in this union, if the ordeal I have suffered is the price. And so I beg of you, Father, that you obtain from the sultan the annulment of our marriage."

Despite the grand vizier's dreams of marrying his son to the princess, he did not think it appropriate, given his son's resolve, to ask him to draw out his patience another few days. He left him and hurried back to the sultan, to whom he confessed that by his son's own account the story was all too true. Before the sultan could talk of breaking off the marriage, which he seemed only too inclined to do, the vizier begged him to allow his son to withdraw from the palace and return home, lest the princess's love for him should expose her to any further anguish.

Prince Aladdin

At once the sultan gave orders to end the celebrations in his palace and throughout the kingdom. Before long, all signs of joy and revelry had ceased. This sudden change fanned speculation in the city: some wondered what mishap had brought on the upheaval, others only noted that the grand vizier and his son were seen leaving the palace with long faces. Aladdin alone knew the secret, and he quietly thrilled at the triumph he owed to the lamp. Strangest of all was that neither the sultan nor the grand vizier, who both had forgotten all about Aladdin and his request, suspected that he might have had a hand in the mysteries that had ended the princess's marriage.

Still, Aladdin let the rest of the three months go by. He counted each day with care, and when they were spent, he sent his mother to the palace to remind the sultan of his promise. In sending her away for three months, the sultan believed he had seen the last of her, for despite the brilliance of her gift, he judged by the plainness and poverty of her appearance that the marriage she proposed was hardly suitable for the princess. Yet here she was, imploring him to keep his word. The sultan, ill at ease, played for time: turning to his grand vizier, he confessed his doubts about marrying the princess to a stranger he supposed to be destitute.

The grand vizier was quick to volunteer his thoughts. "Majesty," he said, "it strikes me that there is one way of avoiding such an ill-suited marriage without giving Aladdin cause for complaint. That is to set the princess at such a high price that his fortune, whatever it may be, could never match it."

The sultan was pleased, and turned to Aladdin's mother. "Good woman," he said, "sultans must keep their word, and I will keep mine, but first your son must send me forty vessels of solid gold, each filled to the brim with jewels, carried by forty black servants, led by as many white ones, all young, tall, well made, and splendidly dressed. I shall await his answer."

Aladdin's mother bowed again before the sultan and withdrew. On the way home, she laughed to herself about her son's wild ambition. "Where will he find all those gold vessels," she thought, "and all that colored glass to fill them? Will he go back to the underground place to pick them from the trees? And all those servants, turned out as the sultan described, where will he get them? Where are his dreams now! I do not expect he will be pleased with my report."

By the time she entered the house, she had convinced herself that Aladdin had nothing left to dream of. "My son," she said, "I would abandon all hope of marrying Princess Badr al-Budur. It is true that the sultan received me with kindness, and I believe he was well disposed toward you. But the grand vizier seems to have turned him, as you may judge yourself by what happened. When I reminded His Majesty that the three months had passed, and begged him to remember his promise, I noticed that he only gave me an answer after speaking for some time with his vizier." Aladdin's mother carefully related the sultan's words, and the precise conditions he had imposed on the marriage.

"He is expecting your answer," she told her son with a smile, "but I think he will be waiting a long time."

"Not so long as you think," replied Aladdin, "and the sultan is mistaken if he believes that his demands will put me off. I had expected real obstacles, but what he asks is very little." He retreated to his room and summoned the jinni.

"The sultan will give me his daughter to marry," said Aladdin, "but first he wants forty gold vessels, full to the brim with fruit from the garden where I found your master the lamp. These forty gold vessels must be carried by as many black servants, preceded by forty white servants, all young, tall, well made, and richly dressed. Go and bring me such a gift without delay, so I may send it to the sultan before the divan session is out."

The jinni returned at once with the eighty servants, each bearing a solid gold vessel on his head, filled with pearls, diamonds, rubies, and emeralds, even larger and more beautiful than those the sultan had seen. Together they filled the small house and its garden. Aladdin opened the door, ushered out the men one after the other, and when his mother had walked out after the last servant, he closed the door behind her and retreated calmly to his room.

The first servant to leave Aladdin's house had amazed everyone who saw him, and before all eighty men were out, the street was full of people running from all directions to catch sight of the procession. The polished skin, the elegant form and carriage of these men, their equal size, their solemn pace, married with the gleam of heavy jewels that hung about their waists and framed their temples, stirred the crowd to a wild delight, but the streets were so packed with bodies that none could move. Only their eyes followed the parade until they could see no more.

Many streets lay between these splendid men and the palace, and half the city saw them pass. When the first of the eighty servants reached the door of the first courtyard, the porters, who took him for a king on account of his clothes, stepped forward to kiss his hem. But the servant, under orders from the jinni, stopped them, and said: "We are but slaves. Our master will appear in time."

The first servant, followed by the others, moved on to the vast second courtyard, where the palace guard stood while the divan was in session. The officers in command of each troop were a spectacular sight, but they paled in the presence of the eighty servants who formed part of Aladdin's gift and bore the rest of it on their heads. Nothing else shone so brightly in the sultan's palace. The brilliance of his court faded before what had just appeared in its midst.

When the sultan heard that these men had arrived, he gave orders to admit them, and they entered the divan in stately fashion, some from the left and others from the right. Once they had formed a great half-moon before the sultan's throne, the black servants laid the vessels they had carried on the carpet, then they all knelt and pressed their foreheads to the floor, and the white servants did likewise. When they rose again, they stood modestly with their arms crossed on their chests, while Aladdin's mother presented them.

"Majesty," she said, "my son Aladdin is well aware that the present he has sent is not worthy of the princess, yet he hopes that you will not be displeased with it, considering that he has tried to conform to the conditions you were good enough to impose."

The sultan barely heard her. A glimpse of the forty gold vessels, brimming with the most vivid and precious jewels, and of the eighty servants who seemed as many kings, had left him speechless. He turned to his grand vizier, who knew no more than he did as to the source of such a cornucopia. "Well, vizier," he said, "what do you make of that man, whoever he is, who sends me such a sumptuous gift, and who is unknown to us both? Do you believe him unworthy of marrying my daughter?"

The grand vizier did not dare dissemble, and the sultan

banished his doubts. He did not even think to discover whether Aladdin's other qualities might make for a suitable son-in-law. The mere sight of such riches, and the diligence with which Aladdin had met his wild request, apparently without the slightest trouble, persuaded him that Aladdin had every accomplishment one could wish for. "Good woman," he said to Aladdin's mother, "go and tell your son that I await him with open arms."

The eighty servants were not forgotten. They were brought inside the palace, and the sultan, after praising them to the princess, had them placed outside her room, so that she could look at them through her latticework screen and judge that he had exaggerated nothing, but rather had told her much less than what was there.

Aladdin's mother lost no time telling her son the good news. "You have every reason to be happy," she said. "Your wishes have been granted. I won't keep you waiting any longer: The sultan has consented to your marrying the princess, and the court applauded his decision. He looks forward to embracing you and concluding your marriage. Now it is up to you to prepare for that encounter, so that the hopes he has placed in you are not disappointed; but after the marvels I have seen you perform, I have no doubt he will be satisfied. Now make haste, my son. The sultan awaits you impatiently."

Overjoyed, Aladdin retired to his room and called the jinni. "Give me a bath," he said, "and when I am clean, find me an outfit more splendid than any monarch has ever worn."

At once he was taken to a bathhouse made of the finest marble, where unseen hands undressed him in a spotless hall. He was led into the bath, which was just hot enough, to be scrubbed and sluiced with scented waters. After passing through a series of further rooms, each cooler than the last, he emerged a quite different man, his complexion now white and pink, his body lighter, refreshed. Back in the hall, he saw that in the place of his old clothes lay an exquisite new outfit, which he put on with the jinni's help, admiring each garment in turn. Then he asked the jinni for a horse more gentle and more graceful than any in the sultan's stables, twenty servants to attend him, six handmaidens to wait on his mother, each bearing an outfit just as sumptuous as any in the sultana's wardrobe, and ten thousand gold coins in ten purses.

The jinni disappeared and returned immediately with the horse, the twenty servants, ten of which carried purses filled with gold, and the six handmaidens, each bearing a different outfit for Aladdin's mother, wrapped in a silver cloth, and presented it all to Aladdin. Of the ten purses, Aladdin gave four to his mother, and left the remaining six in the hands of his servants, with orders to send the coins flying into the crowd as they passed on their way to the palace. At last he presented the handmaidens to his mother, and said that they were hers, along with the clothes on their heads.

Then he mounted his horse and set off to the palace. He had never been on a horse before, yet moved with such grace that not even the finest rider would have guessed he was so green. The streets through which he passed rang with cheers, rising to a roar when the six servants sent handfuls of gold coins flying to the left and right. Aladdin went unrecognized, not only by those who remembered his days of mischief on these streets, but even by those who had seen him not long before, so altered were his looks, for it was a property of the lamp, as it enriched its owners, to match their appearance by degrees to their higher standing. As word spread that the sultan had given Aladdin the princess to marry, he appeared so deserving of the honor that no one thought to doubt his importance.

Aladdin arrived at the palace, where everything was set out to receive him. When he reached the second gate and tried to dismount, as was the custom among viziers, generals, and governors of the highest rank, he was stopped by the chief usher, under orders from the sultan, who led him instead to the threshold of the divan and helped him from his horse despite his protests. Taking Aladdin by the arm, he led him past the other ushers, who framed the entrance in two neat lines, and on to the sultan's throne.

When the sultan saw Aladdin, he was just as amazed by his splendid outfit, richer than any he had ever worn himself, as by his radiant skin, his impressive size, and a certain air of grandeur quite unlike the modest state in which his mother had appeared before him. He rose from his throne in time to stop Aladdin from throwing himself at his feet, embraced him, and led him into a dazzling hall where a feast was laid, and where they ate together alone. The sultan, eyes fixed on Aladdin in delight, let their talk drift over many subjects, and found that Aladdin could speak with knowledge and wisdom on all of them.

After the meal, the sultan summoned the highest-ranking judge in the city, and had him draw up the marriage contract on the spot. Meanwhile, the sultan and Aladdin kept up their conversation in the presence of the grand vizier and the gentlemen of the court, who admired the soundness of his mind, his easy eloquence, and the subtle observations with which he peppered their exchange.

When the judge had finished the contract, the sultan asked if Aladdin wished to conclude the ceremony that day. "First," replied Aladdin, "I beg your permission to build a palace across from yours, so that I may receive the princess in the style she deserves." The sultan agreed, and Aladdin took leave in the manner of one who had grown up entirely at the court.

Aladdin got back on his horse and returned home the way he came, through the same crowds who cheered his passage and wished him every joy. Once home, he took the lamp and said to the jinni: "Build me a palace out of porphyry, jasper, agate, lapis, and marble, and let it stand opposite the sultan's palace. At the top you shall build a great domed hall with walls of gold and silver, and with six windows in each wall. The screen on each window shall be set with diamonds, rubies, and emeralds—except for one screen, which you shall leave unfinished. There must also be a courtyard, a garden, a treasury filled with gold and silver, and kitchens, larders, laundries, dressing rooms furnished for all seasons, stables full of horses with their squires and grooms, and a team of huntsmen. Go, and return when it is done."

A Palace of Wonders

The sun had just set when Aladdin dismissed the jinni. At first light he appeared again. "Master," he said, "your palace is complete." A nod was enough to take them there in an instant, and Aladdin admired every room in the palace, particularly the hall with twenty-four windows, and found there more opulence and beauty than he had dared imagine. "Only one thing remains," said Aladdin, "and that is to roll out, from the gate of the sultan's palace to the door of the princess's quarters in this one, a carpet of the finest velvet." The jinni disappeared, and Aladdin saw that what he had asked for was done.

The porters, who were used to a clear view of the land outside the palace, were amazed to find it cut short, and to see a velvet carpet stretching from the sultan's gate into the distance. Their surprise only grew when they made out Aladdin's palace, and before long news of that wonder had spread through the court. The grand vizier was no less astonished than the others, but when he told the sultan, he tried to pass it off as the work of magic.

"But vizier," said the sultan, "you know as well as I do that Aladdin has built a palace with the permission I gave him in your presence. After the glimpse we have had of his riches, should we be surprised that he has done it so quickly? He has shown us that with enough money, miracles can happen overnight. Your talk of magic is born of some jealousy, is it not?" He was due for a session with the council, and this stopped him from pursuing this thought any further.

When Aladdin came home, he found his mother awake, trying on one of her new outfits. He pressed her to go to the sultan's palace with her new servants as the sultan's council session was drawing to a close, and to say that she had come to keep the princess company until evening, when it would be time for her to move to her palace.

She set out with her women, and though they were dressed as queens, no heads were turned as they passed, for their faces were covered and cloaks hid their sumptuous outfits. Aladdin, for his part, mounted his horse, and, having left his father's house for the last time, carrying only the wonderful lamp which had been so crucial to his happiness, he made for his palace with the same ceremony as before.

As soon as the palace guards saw Aladdin's mother approach, orders were sent to the trumpeters, cymbalists, and fife-players already dotted around the grounds, and in a moment their music sent tidings of joy across the city. Merchants set about decking their shops with carpets, cushions, and foliage, and preparing illuminations for nightfall. Craftsmen abandoned their workshops as everyone scrambled to the main square, which was now wedged between the sultan's palace and Aladdin's. The crowd was bewildered to see a gorgeous palace where the day before there had been no sign of bricks or mortar.

Aladdin's mother was greeted in grand style, and ushered into the princess's quarters by the chief eunuch. The princess embraced her, sat her on the sofa, and, as her women finished dressing her in Aladdin's jewels, had a princely breakfast served. The sultan, who had come to see his daughter before she left his palace for Aladdin's, also gave her a royal welcome. Aladdin's mother had addressed the sultan several times in public, but never before had he seen her uncovered, as she was now. Though she was aging, her features held the shape of her former beauty, and the sultan, who had only ever seen her in the simplest garb, was full of wonder to see her dressed as splendidly as the princess herself. He reflected that this too must be the work of Aladdin's wisdom.

When night fell, the princess took leave of her father.

They parted in tears, and embraced each other tenderly many times, and at last the princess left the palace, with Aladdin's mother by her side and a hundred handmaidens in their wake. They were followed by the musicians, one hundred messengers, and as many eunuchs. Four hundred young pages walked in single file on either side, each bearing a torch which, combined with the palace illuminations, gave a lovely glow to the evening light.

The princess walked the carpet from her father's palace to her husband's, and Aladdin ran to greet her at the door.

"Your eyes are to blame for my boldness," he said, "if I have displeased you."

"Prince," she replied, "now that I have seen you, I submit to my father's will without resistance."

Taking her by the hand, Aladdin led her into a great hall lit by an infinity of candles, where the jinni had laid a sumptuous feast. Gold plates held the finest meats. The vases, bowls, and cups which crowded the table were also made of gold, and exquisitely wrought. The princess said to Aladdin: "I had not thought any place on earth could be more beautiful than my father's palace, but the sight of this room alone proves I was mistaken."

The princess, Aladdin, and his mother took their seats, and a chorus of women began to sing, accompanied by a consort of instruments. The princess, delighted, declared she had never heard anything like it in her father's palace. She did not know that these musicians were sprites chosen by the jinni.

After supper, a troupe of dancers replaced the musicians. They performed a series of traditional dances, and were followed by a man and a woman dancing alone with striking agility. It was near midnight when, true to the Chinese custom, Aladdin rose and offered the princess his hand so that they might dance out of their own wedding. Admiring eyes followed their every turn until they disappeared into the nuptial chamber.

In the morning, Aladdin's servants came to help him dress, and chose an outfit no less fine than the one he wore to his wedding. Then he was brought one of his horses, which he rode to the sultan's palace, surrounded by a flock of servants on all sides. The sultan embraced him, and, seating him beside him on the throne, he gave the order for lunch to be served. "Majesty," said Aladdin, "I beg you to relieve me of that honor today, and instead to give me the pleasure of hosting you in the princess's palace, with your grand vizier and the gentlemen of the court." The sultan agreed, and set off at once on foot, as the journey was not long, with Aladdin on his right, the grand vizier on his left, and the gentlemen in their wake.

The beauty of Aladdin's palace astounded the sultan; inside, he could not keep from exclaiming in every room. When he entered the hall with twenty-four windows, and saw the screens inlaid with diamonds, rubies, and emeralds, and Aladdin remarked that they were just as richly made on the outside, the sultan could do no more than stand there as though stunned. After remaining some time in this state, he said: "This palace is one of the wonders of the world. Where else in the universe are walls built of gold and silver, and windows shielded by screens studded with diamonds, rubies, and emeralds? Never on earth was such a thing ever seen!"

The sultan wished to study the beauty of the twenty-four windows. Counting them, he found that only twenty-three were of the same caliber, and that the twenty-fourth had remained unfinished.

"Vizier," he said, for the vizier had taken it upon himself to remain by his side, "it is strange that such a fine room should have this imperfection."

"It seems," replied the vizier, "that Aladdin was pressed for time, and was unable to match this window to the others."

Aladdin, who had slipped away from the sultan to give a few orders, now returned.

"My son," said the sultan, "this must be the most admirable room in the world. Only one thing surprises me. Was it by accident or negligence that one window was left unfinished?"

"It was by design," said Aladdin. "I told the workers to leave it so, as I wished Your Majesty to have the glory of completing this room, and with it the palace."

The sultan accepted with pleasure and sent for the best goldsmiths and jewelers in the capital.

Aladdin led the sultan into the dining hall. There they were met by the princess, who greeted her father with a happy smile. Two tables heaved under a feast arranged in gold platters. The sultan took his place at the first, along with the princess, Aladdin, and the grand vizier. All the lords of the court sat at the second. The sultan confessed that he had never tasted such delicious fare, and said the same of the wine. Even more impressive were the side tables heavy with vials, bowls, and cups of solid gold, all studded with gems. No less charming were the singers ranged around the room, whose voices mingled in harmony with the music of trumpets, cymbals, and drums that came to them from outside.

As the sultan rose from the table, news came that the jewelers and goldsmiths had arrived. Returning to the hall with twenty-four windows, he pointed out the imperfect one to the craftsmen. "I have called you here to mend this window, and to match it to the perfection of the others. Inspect it, and set to work without delay."

The jewelers and goldsmiths studied the twenty-three remaining windows with great care. When they had consulted each other, and discussed what each might contribute to the task, they went back to the sultan. The first jeweler spoke.

"Majesty," he said, "we are all ready to put our skills at your service, but we lack the materials for the task you require: our gemstones are neither precious enough, nor in sufficient quantity, to match this screen to the others."

"I have all the gems you need," said the sultan. "Come to my palace and take your pick."

The sultan sent for his precious stones, and the jewelers took a great many of them, especially those Aladdin had brought. They set to work with them but made little progress, and had to return many times for more. In a month they had not finished half the work. They had used up all the sultan's gemstones, and even had to draw on the grand vizier's collection, yet all they had to show for it was a half-completed screen.

Aladdin, knowing that their task was in vain, told them not only to put down their tools, but to undo all their work and carry the jewels back. The work it had taken weeks to do was undone in a few hours. Alone again, Aladdin pulled out the lamp, and commanded the jinni to finish the window.

The craftsmen arrived at the palace, and were ushered into the sultan's quarters. The first jeweler, presenting the stones they brought back, spoke for them all: "Your Majesty knows how long we have labored on our task. We were well advanced when Aladdin ordered us to stop, and to undo our previous work and return the gemstones we had borrowed."

The sultan sent for his horse at once and went back to see Aladdin. "I have come in person," said the sultan, "to ask your reasons for leaving such a rare and gorgeous room unfinished." Aladdin concealed the true reason, which was that the sultan was not rich enough in gemstones to finish the screen. Still, in order to impress on him that the palace surpassed not only the sultan's own, but any other on earth, Aladdin answered: "It is true that Your Majesty saw this room unfinished, but I beg you to tell me now if it lacks anything."

The sultan made for the unfinished window, and, finding it just like the others, he doubted his own eyes. He inspected the windows on either side, then all the others, and when he was convinced that the screen which had cost him so many weeks of labor had been perfected in so short a time, he embraced Aladdin and kissed him between the eyes.

The sultan returned to his palace alone the way he had come. There he found the grand vizier waiting for him. Still in wonder at the miracle he had just seen, he recounted it in terms that left the minister in little doubt that things were not as they seemed, and that Aladdin's palace was the work of magic, as he had suggested to the sultan almost as soon as the palace appeared. He tried to repeat himself. "Vizier," interrupted the sultan, "you have made this point before. I see you have not yet recovered from the failure of my daughter's marriage to your son."

The grand vizier, not wishing to confront the sultan, let him think as he pleased. Every morning, on waking, the sultan would look out of the window that gave a view of Aladdin's palace, and returned several times a day to admire it.

Aladdin, meanwhile, did not stay indoors for long. He made sure to be seen by the townspeople at least once a week, either by varying the mosques he attended for prayer, or by calling in on the grand vizier, or by paying the lords of the court, whom he often entertained in his palace, the honor of returning their visit. Every time he went out, he had two servants follow his horse and cast handfuls of gold coins into the crowds as they passed. Not a soul came knocking at his door in need who did not leave satisfied.

As Aladdin went hunting at least once a week, sometimes

in the fringes of the city and sometimes farther afield, he extended his charity to the country lanes and villages. His freehanded manner won him the hearts of the people, and it became common to hear them swear on his head. To these qualities he added a sincere devotion to the welfare of his kingdom, which he displayed when a revolt broke out near the border. On hearing that the sultan had raised an army to suppress it, he begged him to let him take its lead. He prevailed, and marched the sultan's men against the rising, and proved so deft in his campaign that news of the rebels' defeat soon followed that of his departure for the battlefield. He returned a hero, but remained as gentle and gracious as ever.

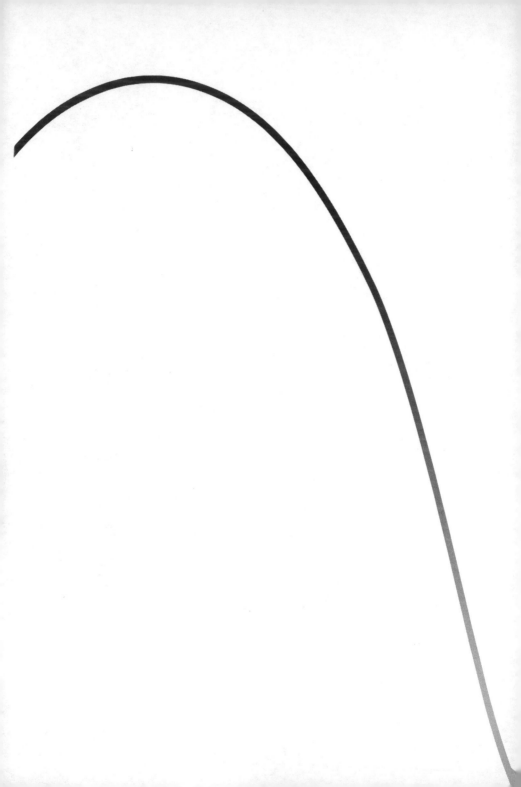

New Lamps for Old

It was years into Aladdin's new life when the magician, far away in North Africa, remembered him. Though certain Aladdin had not left the vault, it occurred to the magician to find out precisely how he had died. Being a skilled geomancer, he took from a cabinet the square box he used in his readings, and, having prepared and leveled the sand, cast the points, and revealed the figures, he found that Aladdin had escaped and had married a princess, with whom he lived in great splendor.

Heat rose to the magician's face. He knew Aladdin could only have survived by the power of the ring, and wasted no time pondering what to do. Next morning he set off on the Berber horse he had in his stable, and traveled day and night until he reached the capital of the Chinese kingdom in question. He dismounted at a khan, or inn, where he took a room for the night.

The next day, he wished to know before all else what people thought of Aladdin. He wandered the city and stopped at a popular meeting place where people gathered to sip a certain hot drink, familiar to him from his previous visit. A cup of the brew was set before him as soon as he found a seat. He kept an ear out and noticed that talk was of Aladdin's palace. Draining his cup, he approached one of those speaking, and asked him what it was about this palace that merited such praise.

"Where have you come from?" said the man. "Have you not heard of Prince Aladdin's palace, the wonder of the world? It is all one talks about on earth since it was built. Go and see it, and judge whether I have told you any more than the truth."

"Forgive my ignorance," replied the magician, "where is this wonder you speak of?"

The other man directed him and he set out at once. When he saw the palace, he knew that it had been built by one of the jinn, who alone were capable of such marvels. Enraged, he determined to get hold of the lamp. For this he shut himself in his room and turned again to geomancy, and the figures revealed to him that the lamp was in Aladdin's palace. He went to see the innkeeper, and, alighting on a perfectly natural pretext for conversation, said that he had just seen Aladdin's palace, and related all that he had found most striking in it.

"Yet my curiosity will not be satisfied," he added, "until I meet the master of such a marvelous place."

"You will have no trouble finding him," said the innkeeper. "Hardly a day goes by when he does not appear in the city. But he has been gone for three days on a hunt that is said to last eight."

The magician waited not a minute longer. He bought a dozen copper lamps, put them in a basket, and took them to the palace. As he approached, he began to call: "New lamps for old!" The children in the square, who thought him mad, ran after him jeering, but he continued to cry: "New lamps for old!" until even Princess Badr al-Budur, who was sitting in the hall with twenty-four windows, heard his voice. She sent a servant to find out what the noise was about.

The handmaiden came back laughing, and the princess scolded her. "Princess," replied the servant, "who could keep from laughing at the sight of a madman offering new lamps for old ones?" On hearing this, another handmaiden said: "There is an old lamp in that alcove which he can have. Then we'll see if he really is mad enough to swap a new lamp for an old one."

This was Aladdin's magic lamp, which he had to thank for the dream his life had become, and which he had left there before setting out on his hunt. The princess, who knew nothing of its value, sent a eunuch to make the exchange.

He went down and said to the magician: "Give me a new lamp in return for this."

The magician had no doubt that this was the lamp he sought. There could hardly be another like it in Aladdin's palace, where everything else was made of gold or silver. He snatched it, and told the servant to take his pick. The square rang out with jeers, but the magician paid them no attention and walked away. He made his way through the backstreets, and in a deserted alley abandoned the basket with its new lamps, as he had no more use for them. Then he left the city gates and pressed on into the countryside. He settled in a lonely place until nightfall, when at last he pulled the lamp from his cloak and rubbed it. The jinni appeared: "What is your command?" The magician asked to be carried, along with the palace and the princess in it, to a certain place in North Africa.

In the morning, the sultan looked out of the window to admire Aladdin's palace and found only empty space. He rubbed his eyes and saw nothing more, though the air was clear, the sky blue, and the early morning picked out all things distinctly. "I am not mistaken," he said to himself. "It stood right there. If it had collapsed, it would still lie there in ruins, and if the earth had swallowed it up, some trace of it would remain."

He sent for the grand vizier, who arrived in such haste that he did not notice anything out of place. But now he, too, was lost in astonishment. Again he put it down to magic, and this time the sultan could hardly argue. "Where is that impostor?" he cried. "Off with his head!"

Thirty horsemen were sent to bring Aladdin back in chains. They met him riding home, five or six leagues from the city. "Prince Aladdin," said the officer, "it is with great regret that we must arrest you and lead you to the sultan as a criminal of the state. We beg you not to think ill of us for carrying out our duty, and to forgive us."

These words startled Aladdin, who asked the officer what crime he was accused of, but neither the officer nor his men could say. As Aladdin saw that his men were out-numbered by the guard, and that some of them had already deserted him, he dismounted. "Here I am," he said, "but know that I am guilty of no crime, neither against the sultan nor the state." A long, thick chain was slipped around his neck and torso, so that he could not move his arms, and he was led on foot to the city.

The people, who loved him, and who saw that he was walking to his death, took up their swords, and those who had none armed themselves with stones, and they went after the horsemen. Soon they had grown to such a number that it was all the guard could do to keep the people from taking Aladdin before they reached the sultan. The men took care to fill the streets they passed, spreading out as they widened and closing ranks as they thinned, and in this way arrived at the palace.

Aladdin was carried before the sultan, who ordered the

executioner to cut off his head. The executioner took hold of Aladdin, removed the chain that bound his body, and, after laying down a strip of hide stained with the blood of a thousand other convicts he had killed, pushed Aladdin to his knees and covered his eyes. Then he drew his sword, sent it flying through the air three times to try its swing, and waited for the sultan's signal.

At that instant the grand vizier noticed that the crowd had overcome the guards and were now scaling the walls of the palace. Just as the sultan drew breath to give the signal, the vizier said: "Majesty, I beg you to consider what you are about to do. You run the risk of seeing your palace stormed, a disaster which could prove deadly."

"My palace stormed!" said the sultan. "Who would dare to attempt such a thing?"

"If you were to cast your eyes down to the palace walls and into the square, you would know the truth of what I say."

Horrified by the unrest in the square, the sultan called for the executioner to stay his hand, had Aladdin unbound, and pardoned him in front of the crowd. Overjoyed to have saved the life of a man they loved, the insurgents relayed the news to those around them, who passed it on to the others beyond. The guards, who had climbed to the highest terraces, made Aladdin's pardon known to the entire city. The sultan's merciful gesture calmed the crowd, eased the turmoil in the square, and sent everyone quietly home.

When he found himself free, Aladdin begged to know his crime. "Do you claim to ignore it?" said the sultan.

"Come here," and he showed him from the window the place where his palace had been. Aladdin looked and saw nothing. There was only empty space, the land where his palace had stood. Unable to guess what had become of it, he was too shocked to say a single word.

"Tell me, then," said the sultan impatiently, "what you have done with your palace and my daughter. The first is of no concern to me, but without my daughter I cannot live. You must bring her back or lose your head, and this time I shall not be stopped."

Aladdin begged the sultan to grant him forty days, promising if he failed to find her that he would go to his death without resistance.

"Your wish is granted," said the sultan, "but do not think you can escape. Wherever on earth you go, I will find you."

The Princess's Revenge

Aladdin left the palace heavy-hearted. With downcast eyes he passed through the courtyards, as the guards, who had been his friends, turned their backs to him. Had they approached him instead, they would not have recognized him; he hardly recognized himself, and was no longer sure of his own mind. For three days he roamed the city like a madman, asking everyone he met where his palace was. Some only laughed at him, but the wisest were moved to pity. He wandered about irresolute, living on the charity of others.

At last he set out for the countryside, and, after crossing

"Now I know the Maghrebi magician is to blame!" said Aladdin. "He is the most deceitful of men. Where does he keep the lamp?"

"He carries it with him in his cloak. Since I have been here, he has tried to convince me that you died by the sultan's hand, that I must break our vows and take him instead as my husband. He likes to add that you are an ingrate and that you owe your fortune to him, but I only reply with my tears. I suspect he intends to sit out my grief in the hope that I will change my mind, and to use violence if I persist."

Aladdin comforted her, and said he would return around noon in a different guise. He traded clothes with a peasant he met on the road, and after walking to the nearest town, bought a certain powder from the apothecary before returning to his palace. The secret door was opened at once, and he went up.

"Princess," he said, "the loathing you bear your abductor will perhaps make it difficult for you to follow my advice. But it is essential that you dissemble if you wish to be delivered from your captivity. Put on your finest dress, and receive the magician warmly when he comes. Tell him you have forgotten me and invite him to dine with you, and say that you wish to taste the wine of his country. He will go and fetch some. Meanwhile, when the table is laid, pour this powder into one of the drinking cups, and tell the handmaiden who waits on you to bring you that cup, filled with wine, on your signal. When the magician returns, after you have eaten and drunk your fill, have her bring you the cup

with the powder and offer to change your cup for his. He
will be too charmed to refuse, will drain the cup to flatter
you, and will die instantly."

"I confess," said the princess, "that I cannot contem-
plate such advances to the magician without shuddering.
Yet what measures would I not take against such a cruel
enemy! I will do as you advise, since my happiness depends
on it as well as yours." When they were agreed, Aladdin
left the palace and spent the rest of the day nearby, waiting for night.

Princess Badr al-Budur, grieving the loss of her husband
Aladdin, whom she loved more out of inclination than duty,
and of her father the sultan, had neglected to look after
herself since that painful separation. She had even forgotten the grooming habits so well suited to her sex, particularly since the magician had first come to see her, and she
learned from her handmaidens, who recognized him, that
it was he who had taken the old lamp in exchange for the
new one, and by that trickery brought about the horror of
her present state. But the chance to seek her vengeance so
much sooner than she had dared to hope made her resolve
to gratify Aladdin, and as soon as he withdrew she had
her women arrange her hair, and picked out the dress best
suited to her purpose. She chose a golden belt studded with
diamonds and matched it to a string of pearls. Her ruby
bracelets set off the splendor of the necklace and the belt.

When the princess was dressed, she consulted her mirror and her handmaidens, and, finding that she had done all

she could to flatter the magician's passion, she sat waiting for him on the sofa.

The magician entered the room with twenty-four windows at his usual hour. The princess rose and received him with smiles, gesturing to the seat she wished him to take, a courtesy she had not yet shown him. The magician, more dazzled by the princess's eyes than by the jewels that framed her, was amazed. Her splendid appearance, softened by a certain graceful air, was so unlike the woman who had greeted him so far that he reeled. First he tried to perch on the edge of the sofa, but, as he saw that the princess would not take her own seat until he sat where she wished him to, he obeyed.

Then, with a look that led him to believe she did not find him so odious as she had previously hinted, the princess spoke. "You are no doubt surprised," she said, "to find me so changed today, but your confusion will perhaps cease when I tell you that I am of a nature so averse to sorrow and to gloom that I try to banish all cares as soon as I find that their cause has passed. I have considered what you told me of Aladdin's fate, and I know that all my tears will not bring him back. That is why, having honored my husband even into the grave, I am resolved to mourn no more, and have invited you to dine with me. But I have only wines from China, and long to taste those of the Maghreb."

The magician, who had given up all hope of gaining the princess's favor, could hardly say a word of thanks without faltering, and, to steady himself, fell on the subject of the wine: he said that of all the Maghreb's blessings, its wine was among the greatest, and none was finer than that of the region where she found herself now, that seven years ago it produced a vintage unsurpassed in quality, and that he had a whole case of it which he had yet to open.

"With my princess's permission," he said, "I will go and fetch two bottles."

"I would not wish to trouble you," said the princess. "Should you not send someone in your place?"

"I must go myself," replied the magician, "for no one else knows where I keep the cellar key, and no one but me knows how to use it."

"If that is so," said the princess, "hurry back."

Drunk on the promise of happiness, the magician flew to his cellar, and the princess, knowing he would be quick, hastened to empty Aladdin's powder into one of her cups. When he returned they took their seats, and the princess drank to his health.

"You were right," she said, "to praise your wine. It is the best I have tasted."

"Princess," he replied as he lifted his own cup, "my wine is made sweeter by your approval. I am pleased," he added after a sip, "to have kept this vintage for such a happy occasion, for never have I tasted anything so fine."

When they had eaten their fill, the princess beckoned to her handmaiden for two more cups. "In China," she said to the magician, "it is customary for lovers to drink to each other's health by exchanging their cups." She presented her cup to him, and reached out her other hand to take his. The magician reciprocated, seeing in this favor the surest sign that he had conquered the princess's heart.

"Princess," he said, "I see that we Maghrebis have much to learn from the Chinese in the art of love. I shall not forget this custom, nor shall I forget that by giving me your cup to drink from, you have restored my hope in a life I would have despaired of, had your cruelty gone on for much longer."

Tiring of these effusions, the princess said: "Let us drink! You may resume your thoughts in a moment," and the magician was so keen to please her that he drained his cup before she had taken a sip from hers. To show his enthusiasm he had tipped his head back to drink, and there he remained for some time after he finished, until the princess saw his eyes roll back in his head, and he died.

The princess had no need to tell her women to let Aladdin in. Her handmaidens had arranged themselves at equal intervals between the dining hall and the bottom of the stairs, so that the secret door was opened almost as soon as the magician fell back.

Aladdin entered the dining hall and said to the princess, who was running to embrace him: "Princess, it is not yet time. Leave me now, as I have more to do."

When he was alone, he went to the lifeless body of the magician, took the lamp from his cloak, and commanded the jinni to return them to China. The palace returned to its position in front of the sultan's palace with only the slightest of tremors.

The sultan, who believed he had lost his daughter, had been inconsolable since her abduction. He hardly slept, and instead of avoiding those places that might remind him of his sorrow, he sought them out. Now it was not just in the mornings, but several times a day that he went to the window whose view he used to admire and stood there in tears, alone with the memory of what he most loved and would see no more. The following morning, he was so wrapped in his own sorrow that he cast only a brief glance at the view. Noticing that the space was filled, he first imagined it to be the effect of mist, but, looking closer, he was in no doubt that it was Aladdin's palace, and the pleasure of that sight chased grief from his heart.

He rode there as fast as he could. Aladdin, anticipating his arrival, had risen at first light, and, having dressed in his finest clothes, saw the sultan arrive. He went down in time to help him dismount. "I cannot say a word," said the sultan, "before I have seen my daughter." Aladdin led him to her, and the sultan covered her in kisses, his face wet with tears. It was a long time before he spoke.

"My daughter," he said at last, "I suspect it is the joy of seeing me again that makes you look as though no evil has befallen you, yet you must surely have suffered. One is not transported, along with one's entire palace, to an unknown place as suddenly as you were without great terrors. Tell me what happened, and conceal nothing."

"Majesty," said the princess, "if I seem well to you, consider that I began to breathe only yesterday thanks to

Aladdin, my husband and savior, whose loss I had mourned, and that the pleasure of seeing him again has restored me by degrees to my former state. The pain I suffered was only that of being wrenched from Your Majesty and from my husband, whom I feared had fallen prey to your rage, innocent as he was. I suffered less from the insolence of my abductor, whose manner I found repulsive but whom I was able to keep at bay by the power I had over him. Besides, I was no more restrained than you see me now. As for my abduction itself, Aladdin played no part: I am the only cause, though I am innocent."

To convince the sultan, she told him how the magician had come disguised as a merchant trading old lamps for new ones, and how easily she had given away Aladdin's lamp, unaware as she was of its secret power; how she and the palace were transported to the Maghreb at once by the magician; how he had been brazen enough to ask for her hand; how she suffered before Aladdin arrived; how, when he did, they plotted together to remove the lamp from the magician; and how they succeeded, thanks to their subterfuge and the drinking cup.

Aladdin had little more to add. "When they let me in through the secret door," he said, "and I saw the traitor lying lifeless on the sofa, I told the princess to return to her quarters with her handmaidens and eunuchs. Alone, I took the lamp from his cloak, and employed the same secret he had used to remove the palace and the princess, to restore them both to their place. If you were to go up to the dining hall, you would see the magician punished as he deserved."

The sultan went up, and when he saw the magician lying dead, his face already livid from the poison, he embraced Aladdin, and announced a feast of ten days. The magician's corpse was taken out and left on a public road to be pecked at by birds and animals. So it was that Aladdin escaped death for the second time, but it was not to be the last.

woman? Her austerity has won the admiration of the whole city. She does not leave her hermitage except for Mondays and Fridays, when she appears in the city and goes about performing charitable deeds, and healing anyone who complains of headache with her hands."

The magician went straight to the hermitage of Fatima the holy woman, as she was known to the city. He had only to lift the latch to enter, and closed the door soundlessly behind him. Inside he found Fatima, lit by the moon, asleep on a thin mat. He held a dagger to her heart and shook her awake. "If you make a sound," he said, "I will kill you, so do as I say."

Fatima, who slept in her habit, rose in terror. "Have no fear," said the magician, "I only want your clothes. Give them to me and take mine." They made the exchange, and he asked her to color his face like hers. Fatima led him into her cell, lit her lamp, and, dipping a brush into a vase, painted his face with its solution. Then she covered his hair with her own headdress, as well as a veil, and showed him how to conceal his face with it when he went around town. At last she slipped around his neck a long rosary which hung down to his belly, and, giving him her walking stick, she led him to the mirror. "Look at yourself," she said, "you are just like me." The magician was satisfied with his appearance, but he did not keep his promise to Fatima, and, not wanting to shed blood by killing her with his dagger, he strangled her, dragged her body by the feet to the cistern in the hermitage, and threw her into it.

Disguised as Fatima, the magician went out into the city the next day. A crowd bloomed around the holy woman. Some asked him to pray for them, others kissed his hand, others only dared touch the hem of his dress, and others offered their bent heads to his hands. He obliged them by letting his fingers float over them, muttering words of prayer, and imitated the holy woman so well that everyone took him for her. After stopping many times to attend to such people, who derived neither help nor harm from this contact with his fingers, at last he reached the square outside Aladdin's palace, where the crowds pressed around him all the more. The strongest and most zealous elbowed their way through the hordes, sending up a cry of indignation so loud that Princess Badr al-Budur, from the hall with twenty-four windows, heard it.

The princess asked what the noise was, and, as nobody could tell her, she sent one of her women to find out. After looking through one of the screens, she informed her that the clamor came from the crowd who surrounded the holy woman, hoping to be healed by her hands.

The princess had long heard of the holy woman's virtues, and dispatched a eunuch to bring her in. When the magician, who hid a demonic heart beneath his saintly cloak, was introduced to the princess, he began by reciting a litany of wishes and prayers for her health, her prosperity, and anything else she might desire. When the deceiver had finished his effusions, the princess said: "My good mother, thank you for your prayers. I hope God will hear them.

Come and sit by me." The dissembler sat down with feigned modesty, and the princess continued: "I have one favor to ask, which you must not refuse me: that is for you to stay with me and tell me about your life, so that I may learn by your example how best to serve God."

"Princess," replied the impostor, "I beg you not to ask such a favor of me, for it would require me to neglect my prayers." "I would not dream of it," replied the princess, "I have many empty apartments: choose whichever suits you best, and use them as you would your hermitage."

The magician, whose only aim was to penetrate Aladdin's palace, where he would be at liberty to carry out his wicked scheme under the protection of the princess, did not resist much longer. He followed the princess, and of all the apartments she showed him he chose the smallest, and said insincerely that it was too good for him, and that he only accepted it to please her.

The princess wanted to bring the holy woman back to the great hall and dine with her there, but, as the magician would have to uncover his face to eat and feared that he would be found out, he begged her to let him take his meal in his room, since he only dined on bread and a handful of dried fruit. After dinner, the pretender joined the princess. "My good woman," the princess said, "how pleased I am that you are here to bless this palace. I shall take you around all its rooms, but first tell me what you think of this hall."

The hoodwinker, who had kept his head bent so far, the better to play his role, at last looked up, and, when he had considered the room, said: "This hall is truly splendid. But in my opinion, worthless as it is, I believe one thing is missing. If this room had a roc's egg hanging from its dome, it would be the wonder of the world."

"Good woman," said the princess, "what sort of bird is a roc, and where are its eggs to be found?"

"It is an enormous bird," said the swindler, "which lives on the peak of Mount Caucasus. The architect of your palace should have no trouble finding one."

The princess could think of nothing but the roc's egg, and resolved to ask Aladdin about it when he returned from his hunt. He had been gone six days, and returned the same evening as the charlatan withdrew to his apartment. As he embraced the princess, it seemed to him that she greeted him more coolly than usual.

"Has anything happened in my absence to upset you?" he asked. "Whatever the clouds hanging over you, there is nothing in my power I would not do to dispel them."

"There is something," said the princess, "but it is very trivial. I believe that our palace is the most splendid that exists on earth, but let me tell you what occurred to me as I examined the hall with twenty-four windows. Do you not think it would be even more perfect if a roc's egg hung suspended from its dome?"

"Princess," replied Aladdin, "you have only to say that a roc's egg is missing from this room for me to find the same fault with it, and to set it right at once."

Aladdin ran up to the hall with twenty-four windows

and summoned the jinni. "What this room lacks," he said, "is a roc's egg hanging from the dome. I ask you, in the name of the lamp, to make up for this deficiency at once."

At that moment the jinni gave such a terrible shriek that the room shook and Aladdin faltered on his feet. "What's that?" roared the jinni. "Is it not enough that I have done everything to serve you? Must I now bring you my master and hang him from the dome of your dining hall? For that outrage, you deserve to be burnt to ashes, along with your wife and the rest of your palace. But you are lucky that this order does not come from you. Its real author is the brother of the Maghrebi magician, who is now in your palace, disguised as Fatima the holy woman, whom he assassinated to take her place! It was he who put that idea into your wife's head. He wants to kill you; it is up to you to save yourself."

With these words, he disappeared.

Aladdin had heard about Fatima the holy woman and her reputation for curing sore heads. He returned to the princess's apartments and said a violent headache had come over him. The princess sent for Fatima. "Come here, good woman," said Aladdin to the fraud. "My head aches. I implore your help and entrust myself to your prayers, and hope that you will not refuse me the blessings you have granted to so many other unfortunates." He rose with his head lowered, and the trickster moved toward him holding a dagger beneath his habit. Aladdin seized his hand before he could raise it, drove the dagger through his heart, and threw him lifeless to the ground.

"What have you done?" cried the princess. "You have killed the holy woman!"

"No," said Aladdin, "it is not Fatima I have killed," and he told her how she had been deceived.

So it was that Aladdin was saved from the two wicked brothers. Some years later, the sultan died at a great age. As he left no sons, Princess Badr al-Budur succeeded him, and shared her power with Aladdin. They reigned together for many years and left behind them a brilliant succession.

Epilogue

"Majesty," said Shahrazad as she finished the tale of the wonderful lamp, "you will have recognized in the Maghrebi magician the mark of a disturbed mind, a man gripped by the mania of wanting things, whose foul methods led him to great riches only to take them away from him, for he showed himself unworthy of them. In Aladdin, on the other hand, you will have seen a man who, though born to a humble home, rose to be king thanks to the same riches, which he acquired without having sought them, and which flowed to him in proportion with his need and his desire.

As for the figure of the sultan, you will have learned from him how even the fairest of monarchs courts danger, and risks even losing his crown, if he dares to act against natural justice, and if intemperate haste moves him to condemn an innocent man to death before giving him his say. You will, in the end, have recoiled from the crimes of the two brothers: one of them paid for his love of gold with his life; the other lost his life and his religion to avenge that villain, and, like him, reaped the reward of his wickedness."

The sultan expressed to Shahrazad, his wife, his great delight at the marvelous workings of the lamp, and the pleasure he took from the stories she told him night after night, for they were enchanting, and almost always underpinned by a useful moral. He could see how deftly Shahrazad spun them one after the other, and did not take exception to these devices, for they allowed him to defer the promise he had so solemnly made, which was to keep each wife for one night only and put her to death in the morning. His only concern, in fact, was that her well of stories appeared to have run dry.

For this reason, having heard the end of the tale of Aladdin and Badr al-Budur, which was quite unlike anything he had heard before, he did not wait for Dunyazad and woke his wife himself as soon as morning broke, and asked her if she had reached the end of her tales.

"The end of my tales!" said Shahrazad. "I am far from it.

Their number is so great that even I would be quite inca-
pable of counting them. My only fear is that Your Majesty
should tire of my voice before I have told them all."

"Banish your fears," said the sultan, "and if you will, tell
me another one."

SELECTED BIBLIOGRAPHY

Dyâb, Hanna. *D'Alep à Paris: Les pérégrinations d'un jeune Syrien au temps de Louis XIV*. Translated and annotated by Paule Fahmé-Thiéry, Bernard Heyberger, and Jérôme Lentin. Arles: Actes Sud, 2015.

Galland, Antoine, trans. *Les mille et une nuits: Contes arabes*, 3 vols. Edited by Jean-Paul Sermain, with an introduction by Aboubakr Chraïbi. Paris: Éditions Flammarion, 2004.

Gerhardt, Mia. *The Art of Storytelling: A Literary Study of the Thousand and One Nights*. Leiden, Netherlands: E. J. Brill, 1963.

Horta, Paulo Lemos. *Marvellous Thieves: Secret Authors of the Arabian Nights*. Cambridge: Harvard University Press, 2017.

Irwin, Robert. *The Arabian Nights: A Companion*. London: Tauris, 1994.

Kennedy, Philip, and Marina Warner, eds. *Scheherazade's Children:*

Global Encounters with the Arabian Nights. New York: NYU Press, 2013.

Marzolph, Ulrich, ed. *The Arabian Nights Reader.* Detroit: Wayne State University Press, 2006.

Warner, Marina. *Stranger Magic: Charmed States and the Arabian Nights.* Cambridge: Harvard University Press, 2011.